FADED
Radiance

T. J HYDE

Faded Radiance
Copyright © 2021 by T. J Hyde

All rights reserved. No part of this publication may be reproduced, distributed, or transmitted in any form or by any means, including photocopying, recording, or other electronic or mechanical methods, without the prior written permission of the author, except in the case of brief quotations embodied in critical reviews and certain other non-commercial uses permitted by copyright law.

Tellwell Talent
www.tellwell.ca

ISBN
978-0-2288-4517-1 (Hardcover)
978-0-2288-4516-4 (Paperback)
978-0-2288-4518-8 (eBook)

Acknowledgements

"Why don't you write a book?" he said. Initially, I laughed and scoffed at the very idea. Write a book. Ya, right! Well... I wrote a book! It is almost too surreal to put into words, and yes, I understand the irony of that statement.

As I look back upon the six-year path this book idea, subsequent writing, and the journey to finally being published took, the realization of this unique accomplishment slowly began to sink in. Never in a million years would I have believed this entire endeavour would have taken place, let alone be released into the world, hoping to be enjoyed. I sit thinking about it with a sense of pride. With that said, here it is!

I mentioned a "he" above. "He" would be someone who significantly influenced me when I lacked guidance and a sense of purpose. After another failed marriage and some dating disappointments, the need to belong, be seen, and maybe even be loved again had become fleeting sentiments. Then I met "him." After our initial online introduction and a few mutual flirtations, he had me at "I am not a knight in shining armour, but I will give you a kiss and a slap on the ass." Romantic, I know. That was the beginning of when I became something to someone; I had a sense of purpose. I mattered.

Today, we remain friends, as our paths took us down separate roads. Despite moving on, the bond of our past, which I am very grateful for, will never be diminished. My own experiences and feelings influenced Jane's character, including my time within the world of BDSM and D/s. Together, we explored, communicated extensively, and found a friendship that grew with trust, honesty, and appreciation. I am not sure I would understand what complete acceptance meant without any fear of judgment or criticism without our time together. Our connection was life-changing for me, and for that, I am profoundly indebted. My past limiting beliefs prevented me from growing, from experiencing the gifts of what actual communication and acceptance enable in any relationship. Their effects are bountiful beyond measure and in so many unexpected ways. It is difficult for me to articulate all the forms within this short acknowledgment, hence the reason for writing my book. Through the characters, I share some of my experiences, feelings, and growth during my journey. We all have a story from which we can learn a lesson or two in the hopes we don't have to learn it again. Stories enable an escape when we may find ourselves lonely, overwhelmed, or lost. I experienced all of those feelings, and with the help of "him," I found a person within myself, who I am proud of, apologize no more for being, and love. Yes, it's true; I love myself. It has only taken me about thirty-five years, but I got there.

So, I say thank you, with all my being, to "Him." Thank you for accepting me, even when I didn't believe much in myself. Thank you for making me smile, laugh and for kissing away my tears. Thank you for reminding me I am a woman and giving me the freedom to express my femininity without boundaries or fear of rejection. Thank you for sharing your desirous, masculine, and genuinely kind self with me.

Thank you for the support of my family and friends, who brought me back to life when I was broken and crestfallen those many years ago. Without their love and encouragement, writing this book, or even living the life I am today, simply would not be happening. I write my first book in your honour. I love you all very much!

I hope *Faded Radiance* sparks an ember in even the darkest of hearts. Know that you matter; you are loved! The only person who needs to understand, and more importantly, believe these things is You. It will take time for your own beliefs to shift and change, enabling you to see your inner light and most lovable self. Allow yourself some grace during your journey, for we all could use some from time to time.

I cannot fully express my gratitude for all my past experiences, and yes, even the challenging and heart-wrenching ones, for what they taught me is invaluable. As I sit here and think back upon those experiences and where I am today, I appreciate the gifts of wisdom and time bestowed upon me as a result. I am happy, and that is all that matters.

Chapter 1

Heavy sigh. "How long do you think tonight is going to take?" Damian asked Jane with an undertone of annoyance in his voice.

"Most likely until the brewery closes around 2 a.m.," Jane said.

Damian flashed Jane an angry look, which left her feeling bewildered. "Why are you so upset? You knew about tonight for months. Do you not want to go with me?"

Damian refused to even look at Jane; he was so pissed off, and no, going to the party tonight was the last thing he wanted to do. With each passing minute, fury quickly turned into resentment towards Jane. She was excited about her best friend Lauren's engagement party. It seemed like that was all she thought about, and it drove him crazy. The constant feeling of pressure to up the ante with Jane was haunting him, giving him nightmares. The last thing he felt like doing was going to the engagement party tonight for a friend Damian couldn't stand. She was an outspoken, entitled, first-class bitch whom he hated and, when it concerned anything about Jane, Lauren always felt she knew better in a motherly kind of way, making up for the one Jane never had. This night was going to be painful.

Jane knew Damian wasn't happy about going to the engagement party with her, but what hurt her most was he didn't care about how much it meant to her that he came. She knew how much Damian and Lauren loathed one another, but for once, Jane hoped he would put their differences aside for one evening, especially since this was a special night.

"Damian, why are you so upset about this party tonight? Talk to me, please?" she asked in hopes of clearing the air so they could enjoy themselves tonight instead of being on edge.

"Jane, you know this isn't my thing. I don't understand why you are forcing me to go. Lauren and I can't stand one another," he harshly snapped at Jane.

Heartbroken, Jane thought to herself the one thing that was most important to her tonight was that he be there for her because he loved her and wanted to be a part of her life. Everything was always a battle when it concerned him and Lauren. "Damian, why are you so angry with me? What did I do wrong?" Jane questioned in frustration and hurt.

Damian sighed heavily. "I don't feel like going to this bullshit party. You know we don't get along; what do you want from me? If you went on your own, we wouldn't be fighting!"

"I don't want to go on my own; I want my boyfriend with me. People would expect us to be going together."

"I don't give a shit what others expect!" Damian yelled at Jane, slamming his hand against the steering wheel.

Jane felt her chest tighten, unable to catch her breath as her eyes blurred with tears. Why did Damian not want to be seen with her? Why was he like this? Knowing she would only be adding fuel to their fight if she pushed more, Jane was afraid, primarily, of what he may say. Despite what she feared, Jane asked anyway, "Are you happy being with me, Damian? Do you see yourself ever wanting to build a life with me?" Instantly upon hearing her words out loud, Jane regretted saying them.

Damian couldn't believe what he was hearing. "Fuck, Jane, seriously?! Swear weddings make women crazy. You are acting crazy!" Then Damian laughed out loud and looked over at Jane. "What? Are you wondering if you and I will get married?!"

Tears welled up as she heard the contempt dripping from each word he said. Jane questioned if there was any future for them, or was she wasting time with someone who wasn't her happily ever after? What was their future together? Was it so wrong of her to want to settle down with someone and have some security in knowing she mattered, she belonged?

An awkward silence remained between them for several minutes when they pulled into the parking lot of the Dark Horse Brewery, much to Jane's relief. Elegantly crafted wood architecture and stonework gave the building a rustic contemporary look, admired by many who came to enjoy the unobstructed bridge views, the Red Seal chef cuisine, and locally crafted beer. On this night, the building looked especially magical with all the twinkle lights, candles, and flowers, creating a beautiful setting for an engagement party, and not just any party, but one for her best friend, Lauren. As Jane got out of Damian's truck, she dismissed the fact he stormed off up the stairs without looking back to see if Jane was behind him or not. Instead, her eyes drank in the fantastic views. She noticed the flickering candlelight from the many lanterns placed on each step as they guided the guests to the main door. Two large floral arrangements full of white and cream shades framed with greenery flanked the entrance inside, filling the air with their botanical efflorescence. From the parking lot, Jane looked up to see the impressive building's large windows draped in yards of billowy white silk, giving the appearance of a dreamlike state as contemporary jazz music serenaded softly in the background. As Jane took in the cityscape's serene view, set aglow by millions of lights and the beautiful dreamlike world of the brewery, she felt like she was in a fantasy. A welcomed escape from her troublesome life for which she was thankful, even if it was just for a few moments in time.

"It's perfect," she stated quietly to herself. However, even as Jane walked up the steps towards the perfect party, she felt deep within her heart that the sadness of her arduous relationship would overshadow any joy this night held and would be anything but perfect. Pausing before walking through the grand carved wooden door, Jane drew in a deep breath and thought to herself, *smile Jane, it will all be fine.* Despite how she was feeling, a smile crossed Jane's lips as she stepped inside the perfect dream that was not hers.

"Jane!" she heard from a very familiar, and not to mention, extremely excited voice— Lauren's—and her friend wrapped her arms tightly around Jane. "Isn't this place gorgeous?!"

But Jane didn't have time to say anything before two equally excited women came up behind Lauren, hugging her and giving Jane a chance to escape their clutches. One of them, Jane recognized as Lauren's co-worker at the marketing firm, having met her at a couple of ladies' night get-togethers Lauren often held. Jane did not recognize the other, a statuesque, confident woman with long, brunette hair and brown eyes, finished off with a great smile. Jane had a sudden wave wash over her, leaving in its wake insecurity and something that even resembled envy, something Jane wasn't proud of, but it was unavoidable, it seemed. Unsure of why she felt this way, Jane decided it was best not to try to figure out the puzzle going on in her mind this night and just put on a smile and try to have a good time.

"Lauren, this place is amazing! How did your wedding planner ever find this place?"

"It was Jane who did." Lauren smiled while reaching for Jane's hand.

"I didn't do much. It just seemed like a great place to have a party," she said shyly.

The stunning woman beside Lauren stated without acknowledging Jane, "Your planner is amazing! The flowers, lights, music are all perfect," she beamed. "We need drinks." Brooke smiled at the girls and took Lauren by her arm, leading her towards the bar and leaving Jane in their wake.

Jane smiled for a brief moment while she pondered whether to go with them or not. It was a time to celebrate, and even though

Jane's head knew this, it was her heart that told a different story. How she wished with all her heart that Damian wouldn't be so upset. She wanted them to plan a future together with some certainty rather than living in limbo and fear. Sadness began to creep its way to the surface again; taking a deep forlorn breath in, Jane headed to the bar to join the girls.

"Come on, Jane, we are drinking champagne," Lauren exclaimed with excitement.

Jane was handed a glass of sparkling wine and looked to Lauren, who couldn't hide her happiness and excitement. A sense of guilt flooded over Jane, and with that in mind, she demanded of herself "enough." Jane lifted her sparkling glass of bubbly with love in her heart for her best friend. She stated, "a toast to an amazing woman whom we all love and adore. I am honoured to be here tonight to celebrate your engagement. I love you both. To Lauren."

The women laughed and drank while hanging around the bar area, and for a short while, Jane forgot about her woes and enjoyed herself.

"Ladies? I hope you are enjoying yourselves this evening. Can I get you anything more to drink?" The voice was deep and polite. Jane could feel the presence of a man standing behind her, but it wasn't a bad feeling, quite the contrary, Jane felt relaxed.

"You should have a drink with us." Brooke got off her stool at the bar, walked over to Gabriel Lockhart, and wrapped her arms around his waist as she leaned her feminine, curvy body into his. "Hi," she said quietly with a hint of flirtation, which seemed to come naturally to Brooke.

Gabriel shifted his body uncomfortably from Brooke's compromising embrace while hoping his embarrassment of her unsolicited show in front of the customers was somehow unseen by them. But he knew his audience, and when his gaze fell upon Jane, it didn't go unnoticed by her.

Instantly their eyes met, turning Jane's face a shade of crimson, much to her chagrin, as she cast her eyes to the floor. He was unquestionably one of the most handsome and intriguing men she had ever seen. In a couple of earlier meetings at the Brewery with Lauren for the upcoming engagement party, Jane had seen Gabriel Lockhart only briefly but was entranced by him each time. Her embarrassment of a schoolgirl crush showed each time, leaving Jane to reprimand herself not to be so juvenile, but it was just too damn hard. He took her breath away and made her heart feel like it was going to jump out of her chest. Despite not being able to hold his gaze, Jane could recall from memory the depth of darkness in his eyes, haunting yet filled with kindness; dark, thick hair kept short; a groomed goatee and mustache; and an olive complexion. Gabriel's commanding presence felt safe and protective to Jane, with all 6'2" height, broad shoulders and muscular build, dressed in a tailored, button-down shirt and dress pants this night, a change from his usual jeans. Any warm-blooded woman in her right mind would be weak in the knees around such a man, and Jane was no exception.

Lauren was excited and happy this night; she no longer wanted to be reserved and wanted to celebrate, calling out, "It's my party!" Laughing as she reached for her glass.

"It's my party, and Gabriel, you must have one with us! Get this man a drink!" She demanded of the bartender as she laughed and threw her hand up in the air while holding a filled champagne glass, spilling some onto Jane's dress and arm.

Jane jumped off her stool as though her seat had just turned to hot embers beneath her. "Oh!" she exclaimed in surprise.

Lauren couldn't contain giggles, and soon the women were all laughing uncontrollably, all but one that is, Jane. "I'm sorry, Jane!" Lauren said as she tried to gain her composure.

Jane didn't say a word as shock and disappointment filled her, and she tried to find something to wipe herself off with, but there wasn't anything within reach. She turned to walk away and find the ladies' room when Gabriel called out "Jane!" making Jane stop abruptly, unable to move.

Lockhart quickly found a towel from behind the bar and was by Jane's side, taking her hand in his. He slowly began to wipe the champagne droplets from Jane's arm as he gently held her hand. His hand was tender and warm, and yet, Jane still could not manage to meet his gaze while he helped her. As she stood beside him, Jane felt small with her slight frame in comparison to his height. A moment later, a server came over and handed Gabriel a bottle of soda water. He let go of Jane's hand and said, "Take this and see if you can remove the stains."

Jane smiled slightly and quietly replied, "Thank you."

Feeling deflated, Jane dabbed at the stain on her dress alone in the bathroom. Tonight was a celebration for Lauren and Steve's engagement, but instead, it was one of painful ponderings for Jane. Damian was not happy being with her; Jane reluctantly knew this deep down. But like anyone who faced something they didn't want to acknowledge or, more so, deal with, sooner than later, that once-tucked-away problem would rear its ugly head. Jane's heart was heavy from the sheer weight of the sorrow, which became suffocating. Despite the constant reminders of dislike and distrust that Lauren and other friends had for him, her love for Damian was unwavering. Jane knew Damian was uncompromising about marriage and a family of their own one day, but Jane's heart was unwilling to acknowledge this fact. Instead, she lived in a state of disbelief with the hope he would change his mind. There was never a time Jane didn't believe Damian wouldn't be a part of that happiness until this night. As she worked on the stain, Jane could no longer hold back her emotion. Each tear felt like a piece of joy tumbling away as sobs heaved from her chest.

Jane realized her efforts to remove the stain were futile and rested her hands on the counter. *What a mess!* she thought to herself as her reflection in the mirror stared back at her. Mascara streaked down her cheek, and her dress had a very noticeable wet stain. *God, Jane, could you be any more of a disaster?!* She took a tissue in the hope of fixing her smeared makeup, but as Jane looked in the mirror, all she saw was a lost and heartbroken mess. It was no use; there wasn't anything more she could do. Moments later, Jane rejoined the party and scanned the room for Damian. She found him sitting alone at the bar on his phone. A deep sigh filled her chest as she made her way to him.

"Want some company?" she asked hesitantly with a smile.

"Jesus, Jane, what did you do?" he demanded of her, ignoring her question.

"There was a champagne incident and so…" her voice trailed off as she smoothed the front of her dress with her hand and cast her eyes to the floor, somewhat ashamed. "I didn't…" she began to say when Damian looked at his phone and started typing a message. Feeling awkward and unsure of what to do, she decided to sit down beside him.

"So, you might have to get one of your friends to take you home. I'm waiting to hear back from the guys about meeting up for a beer.

"You're going to leave?"

"You know I hate things like this. I don't know why you insisted on me coming when I am not having fun or feel comfortable being with your friends."

Jane didn't know what to say to change his mind, which would only make him angry. Damian was going to exit the party, leaving her alone where their friends were. "Please don't leave, Damian," Jane begged. "Please stay. We don't have to stay much longer. Dinner is soon, and then we can leave." She tried to come up with compromises that may appeal to him in the hopes of him staying longer. But Jane knew deep down, based on how their relationship had progressed over the last while, there wasn't a compromise that would satisfy him. She always felt like she couldn't do anything right around him. He was leaving, and there was nothing she could do to change that.

"Jane, I am not staying here!" He raised his voice, causing a few guests to pause their conversation and look in their direction.

Jane's face flushed with embarrassment and uncertainty at that moment. Speechless, she didn't know what else to do other than to nod, as she desperately wanted to avoid the prying eyes of the party guests, no doubt waiting for a dramatic ending to their quarrel. But Jane wouldn't give them the satisfaction and instead decided she needed to find a quiet escape.

As predicted, Damian left without saying anything to Jane, barely glancing at her as he walked past and left out the front door.

Gabriel heard a man raise his voice, and he saw Jane leave the bar with a look of sadness clouding her pretty face as Damian left, dismissing Jane as he walked past her. Although he didn't know what had transpired between the couple, he did know one thing: Damian was arrogant, and that personality quality infuriated him. For the life of him, Gabriel couldn't understand what Jane saw in Damian, but, like so many other women and men in relationships where one is emotionally and or physically controlling, most partners do not leave. Gabriel shuddered with frustration in knowing Jane was one such person; she deserved so much more. He suddenly realized he was affected by Jane, taking him by surprise, leaving him with one question, "Why did he care?"

The heaviness in Jane's chest made it challenging for her to talk to the coat check attendant. The sadness was all-consuming. Being unable to face anyone, she needed to get outside and escape the happy party atmosphere, if even for a short time.

The fresh, crisp air went unnoticed by Jane as tears streamed down her face, and sobs escaped her chest. She was unfamiliar with the brewery grounds but hoped to find a quiet place to be alone. In haste, Jane followed a sidewalk lit up with lights to escape the hurt and sadness imprinted upon her heart as Damian's words echoed in her mind. Every word he said felt like a dagger plunged into her chest, one she couldn't dodge, that was until she found a lovely garden area where the trees adorned in a soft glow from the twinkle lights welcomed her. Even in her sorrow, Jane couldn't help but admire the beauty surrounding her; it was as though the heavens blanketed the grounds with their love and light, making it feel safe and peaceful away from the commotion of the party. A small fire pit provided some warmth while the flames danced about, lolling Jane away from the feelings of being unloved and rejected. Her tears, which flowed freely moments before, paused as she took comfort in the soothing embrace and solace of her surroundings while breathing in the cool night air.

Jane recalled a time when she and Damian were happy and loving towards one another. Affectionate in their kisses, consumed with one another, unable to keep their passionate need tamed. Jane closed her eyes while the fire crackled in the background, and a memory from several months ago surfaced. Damian came home from a hard day at work, and, being sweaty and dirty from the labour-intensive work, he got into the shower. She saw Damian's naked body blanketed in steam through the glass shower, with the water massaging every ripple of his muscular body. Jane couldn't help feeling aroused at the mere sight of his nakedness. Her own body ached to be touched and teased while being filled with every thrust, waiting in anticipation of Damian's orgasmic moans, feeling his cum's warmth within her, then trickling down her thighs.

Damian loved being dominant, taking Jane as he wished, fisting her hair in his hand while fucking her from behind as he pushed her body up against the glass. Holding her tightly and pulling her body closer to him until their bodies shuddered at their climax felt erotic to Jane. Often Damian whispered, "I needed that," as he held her by her hair or around her neck, ensuring Jane she knew she was his. As Jane reminisced about their past relationship, she didn't see it at the time; however, this night, Jane couldn't help but realize it was just a role to him. He needed to dominate her at his whim, for his pleasure, not for love. The only problem was, Jane had invested her heart into him and their relationship for so long, she believed it was love they shared. Did he love her at all? Did he see any future with her? Tears soon trickled down Jane's face while her heart hurt and her mind tried to reason with it in the hope of making the sadness less burdensome. But then, suddenly, Jane jumped away from her thoughts, realizing she wasn't alone in the garden after all as the sound of footsteps drew closer. She heard her name called out faintly, but Jane remained hushed. Quickly standing up from the bench as her heart raced with anticipation or perhaps relief, Jane whispered to herself, "Damian." Leaving nothing to chance, he may have realized just what she meant to him and had come to tell her how sorry he was; Jane swiftly wiped away her tears with the sleeve of her coat, calling out loud, "Damian?"

The person in the shadows slowly moved into the light, casting a shadow upon the path, making Jane's heart race with angst. To her astonishment, a tall, dark-haired man emerged from obscurity, immediately rendering Jane speechless in bewilderment and unable to move from where she stood before she heard her name called out once again.

"Jane. It's Gabriel."

Chapter 2

"Mmm, that was delicious!" One dinner guest licked her fork clean of the velvety goodness of the chocolate cheesecake. Lauren smiled at her guest, but something seemed off as she looked around the room; her best friend was absent. *Where is Jane?* she thought to herself. It was unlike her to miss the dinner; something was wrong, and Lauren's concern grew. She excused herself from the table and found a quiet space to try Jane's cell. Lauren dialed Jane's number, but it went directly to voicemail. She hung up and sent a text.

Jane, where are you? Is everything ok?

Lauren paced the quiet area as she waited for Jane to message back, but Lauren knew something was wrong as the minutes went by. She walked towards the bar area to round up some help to find Jane and saw Brooke talking with another guest.

"Brooke! Have you seen Jane? We are going to be doing speeches soon, and I can't find her. She wasn't at dinner, and she hasn't replied to my text message. She better not bail on her speech!" Lauren said in annoyance as she thought about how this night was supposed to be perfect.

Brooke didn't answer Lauren's question but instead asked, "I was wondering if I could talk to you for a moment?" She couldn't help but notice Brooke seemed a bit irritated; maybe it had to do with Jane. Lauren knew Brooke wasn't Jane's biggest fan.

"Brooke?" Lauren asked.

"It's silly. You should probably forget about it," Brooke said sheepishly. Despite what Brooke said, though, Lauren saw Brooke was troubled with something.

"Brooke, clearly something is bothering you," Lauren said to her, making it difficult for Brooke to ignore her friend.

"I think he likes her. I caught the two of them trading glances with one another. She likes him, and I think he likes her too. I told you it was silly. Forget it."

But Lauren wasn't about to "forget it" as it was something to Brooke. But she was confused. "Brooke, who is Jane interested in?"

Tears welled up in her eyes as Brooke said, "Gabriel."

Lauren hugged her friend and said, "You aren't silly. But what makes you think they like one another? Have you seen them together or anything suspicious between them? It isn't like Jane to be like that. You know she is crazy about Damian. Have you talked to Gabriel or Jane about it?"

Brooke laughed. "No, it would just make me look jealous."

"I think Jane and Damian are having problems again, like that is anything new," Lauren snidely stated while rolling her eyes. "He isn't good enough for her and only creates drama. It pisses me off; she can't seem to leave him. Jane was upset earlier tonight, and I have no doubt it is Damian's doing. Maybe Gabriel knows why or what happened and is being supportive. I don't know what else to say, Brooke. I don't think he is interested in her in a romantic way. You know Jane is soft-hearted; she isn't as strong as you and I. Maybe he pities her, even though she brings it onto herself, being with such an ass. Lauren paused briefly, then suggested, "Maybe you should go talk to Gabriel, given how much it is bothering you."

Brooke sighed heavily and replied, "I know." And she did. She knew she needed to talk with Gabriel and see for herself if there was any interest in Jane. She shook her head in disbelief at the idea of a sophisticated, successful man like Gabriel Lockhart having any interest in a woman who was barely noticeable and quickly forgotten. Brooke had a great job with a title and the probability of a promotion to move up the advertising ladder, not to mention she was attractive and confident. Her mind tried to spin a logical reason for Gabriel's probable interest in Jane; she couldn't help but wonder, why was Jane so appealing to Gabriel?

Lauren was whisked off by some party guests for pictures, leaving Brooke alone with her thoughts. She looked around the restaurant but didn't see any sign of Gabriel. Brooke checked the kitchen, then his office, but still no Gabriel.

"Hey girl, you need a refill," a guest chimed to Brooke as she walked towards the bar. She decided a refill on her wine was in order, considering how she was feeling.

"Thank you," Brooke said to the bartender, then walked outside to the deck where some of the guests mingled near a beautifully rustic stone fireplace. Drawn to the coziness of the warmth and incandescent glow, Brooke gazed into the flames, preoccupied with thoughts of Gabriel and Jane.

Unaware of time passing, Brooke stood up and walked towards the railing, feeling the warmth on her back while she enjoyed her wine and took in the beautiful view of the garden. It was a large treed area with benches around a fire pit. Hundreds of twinkle lights adorned the surrounding trees, reminding Brooke of the clear, starry night sky. It was as though the stars had fallen and found their place in the trees, giving the garden a peaceful essence. Brooke looked out across the area when something caught her attention. Two people were sitting close together on a bench, cloaked in shadows from the trees. She couldn't take her eyes off them.

Although there was no physical contact between them, they appeared to be talking. But then something piqued Brooke's interest, a familiarity of the couple which quickly forged her out of her dreamlike state. "Oh my god!" Brooke said out loud in disbelief; it was Gabriel and Jane. He sat beside her as she had her head in her hands. Why? Why was he with her in the garden? "You have got to be kidding me!" Brooke wasn't sure what she was going to do or say, but she needed to confront them. She turned and ran down the stairs from the deck to where they sat. Quietly, Brooke approached so as not to give away her presence. In the shadows, she waited to make her move.

"Thank you for talking to me. I'm sorry to have caused you concern," the familiar voice that was Jane's said.

"I wasn't sure if you were ok and wanted to make sure you were," the very recognizable voice of Gabriel replied.

Brooke had enough; it was time to confront them, and she stepped out into the light. "There you are. I've been looking all over for you," Brooke said with her eyes fixed upon Gabriel.

Gabriel smiled as she stood and reached out for Brooke's hand, saying, "Hi." But Brooke immediately stopped short of his reach.

"Why are you out here together?" Brooke demanded, shifting her gaze from Gabriel to Jane. Her glare was cold and her body rigid, closed off, as she crossed her arms across her chest.

Jane felt the sting of Brooke's anger and fidgeted from the usual discomfort she couldn't seem to avoid with Brooke. "It was my fault. I needed some air, and he saw I was upset and came to see if I was ok."

Brooke saw Jane was upset, as Lauren suspected. But that didn't factor into Brooke's annoyance.

Gabriel turned to Brooke and, in a low tone, so as not to cause a scene from possible onlookers from the deck, said, "Damian left Jane here with no way home. I came out to ensure she was ok."

Jane stood up, wiped her face quickly of any remnants of her tears, and decided it was time to leave. She paused beside Brooke and whispered, "I'm sorry. I didn't mean to cause a problem for you both." Then she began walking towards the path as Brooke called out.

Brooke's eyes stayed focused on Gabriel, and without emotion, she said, "Jane? Lauren was looking for you."

Jane glanced back at Brooke, feeling her animosity towards her, and decided it was best not to say anything more. She continued to walk towards the main building to find Lauren.

Gabriel approached Brooke. "I know you are upset, but I don't understand why."

Brooke relaxed her arms and walked to the bench, suddenly embarrassed by her insecurity. "I didn't understand why you were out here with Jane. I didn't realize you knew her that well."

"I saw her leave, and she seemed very troubled. A guest overheard Jane and Damian argue, and I wanted to ensure there wasn't a problem I would have to deal with. That is when I saw Damian leave. From what the guest said, it sounded like he was verbally hostile towards Jane, and that concerned me."

"Damian is such an ass," Brooke stated matter-of-factly. "Everyone knows that about him."

Gabriel knew this was Brooke's way of apologizing and decided to let it go. He wrapped his arms around Brooke and kissed her as a reminder he was there with her. "Thank you for your understanding," he said with a smile.

Brooke shivered in Gabriel's arms, suggesting dismissively, "Let's go back inside." She was relieved Jane was leaving, and soon they could get back to the party and not focus so much upon the helplessness of a woman Brooke struggled to like. "We can talk later about things."

Gabriel heard the tone in her voice and didn't appreciate it but decided to let things go for the moment. He did nothing wrong, and Brooke would need to get her insecurity under control. Drama never played a role in his life, and it wasn't going to start now. But this was neither the time nor place to talk.

The evening had finally come to an end as the guests had their fill of delicious food, drinks, and lots of laughs. As guests called it a night, Jane thanked them for coming and handed out a small gift from the engaged couple. But her mind wandered between thoughts of her fight with Damian and the trouble she caused

Brooke and Gabriel. It didn't seem to matter what Jane did this night; no one was happy with her. The weight of her guilt had her feeling weary as she thought about how heavenly it would feel to be kicking off her heels and curling up in the warmth of her bed. But Jane knew going home would be anything but easy and peaceful; she and Damian had a lot to talk about, given how things went earlier in the evening as her worry smothered any shred of hope for a non-confrontational outcome.

"Thank you, girl, for everything you did tonight," Lauren excitedly said as she threw her arms around Jane.

"I'm sorry for the drama tonight with Damian. Hopefully, not many people saw us argue." But the truth was Jane knew several guests did see them, and her eyes misted over.

"Oh, please don't cry, Jane. It's not a big deal. Everyone had a great time," Lauren said as she wiped away the tears from Jane's cheek before giving her a much-needed hug.

The overwhelming embarrassment had Jane teary. "It's just so embarrassing. Tonight was a party and was supposed to be fun, not about my drama with Damian. I am so sorry, Lauren." She hugged her best friend back tightly.

Lauren stepped back, holding Jane by her shoulders. "We are good. Ok? Go home, get some rest, and talk to him. Things will be ok."

Jane smiled slightly, but deep down in her heart, she knew things were far from being ok.

"Your cab is waiting for you, Jane," she heard Brooke say behind her. "Gabriel called one for you," she stated flatly as she leaned against the wall with her arms crossed, avoiding any eye contact with Jane.

"Oh, ok. Can you tell Gabriel thank you for me?" Jane asked while she put on her coat.

"Sure," was all Brooke said with a hint of annoyance in her voice.

Jane felt relieved for some quiet space away from everyone as she sat in the back of the taxi. Soon she would be home, and hopefully, she and Damian could talk. A glance at her phone showed no word from him at all, leaving her heartsick. Sorrow vanquished the slightest hint of hope she held within as tears welled up in her eyes. She messaged,

I'm on my way home. XOXO.

But it went unread. Why was he ignoring her? How she wished she could turn back the hands of time and change the circumstances between her and Damian, but it was wishful thinking.

Jane's phone chimed with a new text message as she paid the cab driver. "Home," she whispered to herself, and a sigh of relief washed over her while she walked towards the darkened condo. Hopeful, Jane looked at the message, but it wasn't from whom she hoped. Instead, to her surprise, it was from Gabriel Lockhart. His message was sincere, and immediately Jane felt gratitude for his concern. As they had talked in the garden, Jane felt like she was a whiny, insecure girlfriend. Although Gabriel never once made her feel like she was, she couldn't help but wonder what he thought of her. They barely knew one another, yet she'd bared her soul and exposed her heart tonight to a virtual stranger. How would she ever face him again? Then there was the fact he was dating Brooke; no doubt in Jane's mind, she would find out what they had talked about. Jane shook her head and sighed. "Ugh!" The ugly truth was she felt heartbroken and alone. The party was supposed to be spent with Damian and their friends celebrating Lauren and Steve's engagement. Instead, it turned out to be a night of feeling invisible and unwanted.

Gratefully, Gabriel provided Jane a brief moment to vent; however, despite their talk, Jane remained preoccupied with her problems and couldn't help but wonder what was going on with Damian as she walked to the front door. Why would he not answer her text messages? His parking space was vacant and total darkness greeted Jane as she stepped inside their condo. Jane's mind raced with what-if scenarios when a sudden feeling of nausea hit her like a ton of bricks. Maybe it was something she ate or drank at the party, Jane wondered as she stumbled down the darkened hallway towards the bathroom.

A few minutes later, Jane lifted herself off the bathroom floor and turned on the light; its harsh brightness was too much, and she quickly covered her eyes with a hand. Slowly, Jane opened her eyes and caught sight of a woman with mascara-smudged eyes staring back at her in the unforgiving mirror. She quickly averted her gaze from the reflection. Jane barely recognized herself as she washed her face of all evidence of her despair. But she could not contain her tears any longer or stand the sight of herself as she shut the light off and sat down on the edge of the tub, alone in the dark.

The stillness of the darkness felt comforting as Jane took advantage of the quiet time to think without distraction. Thoughts of Damian and their recent problems compounded her feelings of lonesomeness. The truth was unyielding and unavoidable: Jane was alone and unloved. Tears trickled down her cheeks as she thought about how Damian was her everything, yet she wasn't his. Their relationship was not enough for him, and she wasn't the woman he needed anymore. The very idea of him not loving her burrowed deep within her chest, making it almost impossible to breathe. She was overwhelmed with grief as her heart shattered into pieces with the realization that she wasn't loved by the one man to whom she gave all of herself.

Numbness in her legs subtly reminded Jane to get up. Feeling weary, she crawled into bed in the hopes of hiding from the world, but she could not shelter herself from the daunting sadness which filled her heart as she recalled the memories of the evening's events. Jane held onto a sliver of hope, a hope created out of the love she had for Damian, a hope she would hear from him. However, when she checked her phone one last time before calling it a night, there still was no word from him, only the unread message from Gabriel. She looked at his text and felt a need to show her appreciation for his kindness that evening but hesitated briefly to contemplate what to say. Jane began with,

Thank you for your concern...but quickly changed her mind, erased it, and typed instead,

Home safe. Thank you for the talk.

Satisfied with her reply, Jane drew the blanket up around her as her eyes grew heavy, soon drifting off to sleep, alone.

Gabriel heard his phone notification chime with a message from Jane. Although her reply was brief, he appreciated it nonetheless. He wondered how she was doing after the party and their talk. With Jane being so unsure of herself and insecure about her position in her relationship with Damian, Gabriel knew she wasn't someone who would just let things go. The overthinking was his concern, but he knew Jane would find a way to overcome the fortune-telling thoughts about losing her relationship, which was all based upon fear and insecurity. Because of her limiting beliefs, Jane was blind to her inner strength, something Gabriel knew she would find in time. She deserved to be happy, but first, she had to discover it in herself before seeking it from others, which she often did. Jane needed to understand her value and worthiness weren't found in Damian or any man, for that matter.

As Gabriel looked at the time, he said quietly as he typed a reply,

"Good night, Jane."

"There you are," a familiar voice broke the silence within Lockart's office. "Whatcha up to?"

Gabriel turned in his high-back leather chair to see Brooke standing in the doorway. He smiled, and as he got up and walked towards her, said, "I just messaged Jane to make sure she got home ok." As he was about to embrace Brooke in his arms, she pushed his hands away and walked past him. "Brooke, what's wrong?"

Brooke looked at Gabriel in anger. "Why would you message Jane at all? And why were you two in the garden together?"

Gabriel nodded with understanding. He knew Brooke had fears and doubts despite her outwardly strong and confident appearance. She deserved an honest answer; Brooke should know the truth even if it meant he might betray Jane's confidentiality and trust. "Jane and Damian argued, and she was upset, so I checked on her to make sure she was ok. That is all Brooke. I thought she could use a friend."

Deep down, Brooke knew his heart was in the right place, but she could not fathom someone like Gabriel being attracted to a woman like Jane. Brooke's opinion of Jane was that she was weak and insecure. As this thought seared through her mind, Brooke couldn't admit to herself that Gabriel may have been a friend to Jane, but was he someone who could be something more to her? She could feel the tears of frustration and anger mist over her eyes; that was the last thing she wanted him to see from her. In Brooke's mind, crying was a sign of weakness and a clear sign of a loss of control. The last thing Brooke would allow Gabriel to see was her fear of losing him to a woman like Jane. It simply would not happen. As her fearful thoughts swirled, Brooke let out a deep sigh and walked towards the door. Before opening it, Brooke said flatly over her shoulder, "I'll call you in the morning."

"Brooke, why don't you stay the night with me?" Gabriel stated as he began to walk towards her. But he stopped as Brooke raised her hand to stop.

"No, I need some time to myself. Seeing you with Jane was hard. I want to be on my own tonight."

"Ok," Gabriel replied, choosing not to try and convince her otherwise, so he said instead, "Please let me know you got home safely."

Brooked opened the door and stated, "I will."

Gabriel sat on the edge of his desk and looked out at the gorgeous view of the bay lit up by the lights of the traffic crossing the bridge into the busy city centre skyline. Despite his talk with Brooke, Gabriel had to be honest with himself: he felt compelled to help Jane, or at the very least, to be a friend when she needed one. She was a strong woman with a kind, feminine heart, something he knew Brooke saw as a weakness, judging Jane and being unaccepting of what made her beautiful. Maybe that was what intrigued him most about Jane; he admired her inner strength and vulnerability.

Chapter 3

In the weeks following the engagement party, Jane felt as though her life was on a repeating loop: numerous lonely nights, getting up, going to work, coming home, and going to bed, all the while thinking of Damian. The countless hours of overthinking and worrying about her future with Damian consumed every moment she was awake and haunted her dreams every night. Her attempts to connect with him were challenging; if they weren't arguing incessantly, he was absent, avoiding Jane by being out most nights. Where he went or who he was with were questions Jane knew she wouldn't ever get him to answer. Anytime she tried to talk to Damian about where he would go, he'd smirk and say, "I can go out when I want and see who I want." Then Damian would leave and sometimes not return for a couple of days. There never seemed to be love in his eyes or kindness in his voice towards her; instead, he was callous and distant, even cruel at times. He once loved her, but Jane wasn't sure when that all changed. What happened? Whatever she had done or said, something had changed inside Damian. The man she had fallen in love with didn't exist anymore, and it ripped out her heart.

It seemed her only refuge was work. Extra shifts enabled an escape from her troubles. However, the more Jane lied to herself about the state of her relationship with Damian, the more it made things worse within her heart and soul. She needed help. She needed to talk to someone. With Lauren, though, Jane feared one thing: to hear "I told you so" from her closest friend. But Jane knew she needed support and reached out to Lauren anyway.

With a heavy sigh, Jane nervously waited for Lauren to meet her in the hospital cafe. She wasn't sure why she felt so nauseous while she sat on her own. It seemed since the party, nausea would come and go. But something felt different this time; a sharp pain in her abdomen took her breath away, but as quick as it came on, the pain went away. Maybe it was from nerves or how tired Jane felt. Damian hadn't come home in a few days since their last argument. Perhaps she should have called in sick from work; however, it was probably just all the stress over the last while and nothing more. *Maybe this wasn't a good idea. Maybe I should cancel.* Suddenly, a wave of nausea and abdominal pain washed over her, causing Jane to sit in the chair and close her eyes as she took some slow breaths, hoping it would all pass. Slowly the pain subsided, and the nausea eased just as a familiar voice rang out.

"Hi, sorry, I'm late. My meeting ran longer than expected." Lauren greeted her friend with a hug. "Oooh, you are a lifesaver. Thank you for the coffee."

Jane smiled, "You're welcome. Thanks for seeing me."

"Of course. You haven't been yourself lately. I'm worried about you, Jane." Lauren said as she took her friend's hand in hers. "What's going on? Why have you been distant?

Jane couldn't help but notice the pity in Lauren's eyes and quickly diverted her own to avoid the uncomfortable feeling she felt. The truth was she already knew what Lauren was going to say, and Jane knew she could barely dare herself to face that certainty.

"You look so tired. Are you sleeping?

"Not much since the party," Jane said quietly as she played with her coffee cup.

"We've hardly talked since the party. What's been happening between you and Damian?" Lauren asked.

"I know," Jane said as tears welled up in her eyes. "Lauren… I don't know what to do. Damian and I are not doing well." Jane bowed her head in shame as tears streamed down her cheeks and sobs heaved from her chest. "He's hardly ever home; he never messages anymore, and we argue when he is around. I don't think he loves me anymore." As soon as the words left her mouth, her chest tightened as the heartbreak crashed down upon her.

"Jane, I am so sorry," was all Lauren could come up with. What could she say to make her troubled friend feel less tortured and sad? There were no words that would ease her pain, and she decided just letting Jane cry quietly was the best thing she could do.

A short distance away, at the security desk, the handsome guard sat and couldn't help but notice the pretty woman crying. He recognized she was a nurse at the hospital who always smiled or said hello as she walked by. For months he had waited for her to walk in the doors of the hospital and smile. But on this day, she sat crying, and it touched him to see how sad she was. Picking up a box of tissue, he walked over to where the two women sat.

"Excuse me, sorry, I don't mean to interrupt. Just thought you might need this," putting the box of tissue on the table. Jane recognized the security guard but kept her face down. She was far too embarrassed by the ugliness of her tears and the feelings welling inside her.

"Thank you," Lauren said back to him. I'm Lauren." And she held out her hand.

"Justin. I hope everything is ok," he said as he shook Lauren's hand.

"It will be. Thanks," Lauren stated.

"Ya, no worries, I should be getting back to the desk," Justin said before he turned around and walked back to the desk.

Jane wiped away her tears and smiled at Lauren. She was grateful to her dear friend for being there for her. "I'm not sure where to begin," Jane said as she played with a tissue in her hand.

"Well, let's start from when you were at the party. Brooke told me a couple of days after that Damian left you there. What happened?"

"It started before the party when we were getting ready," Jane recalled. She told Lauren how Damian was upset that he had to go to the party when they were getting ready. To Jane's relief, Lauren remained quiet and just let her talk. She continued to go into detail about their argument after the dinner, where several guests overheard Damian's unkind words, which inevitably ended with how Damian left her at the party to find her way home. "I'm really sorry we almost ruined your party. I didn't expect him to behave like that. He wasn't interested in talking to anyone and kept looking at his phone. Every time I try talking to him about it, he gets mad and leaves. It has been that way for the last couple of weeks." Jane paused a brief moment to catch her breath and weigh out Lauren's reaction to everything she just told her. But still, Lauren just listened. Jane had hoped all of the tension would subside after she had gotten it off her chest, but the feeling of being unloved by the man she adored with all her heart remained ever prevalent.

It was hard for Lauren to see Jane so heartbroken with her every word. There were simply no words to comfort Jane, as the weight of her despair became unbearable. All Lauren could do was stand up from her chair and hug her best friend tightly with love. While she held Jane, Lauren felt anger simmer in her towards the man who carelessly hurt her best friend. It was well known that Lauren never liked Damian and always thought he was never good enough for Jane. She was kind, a little naïve, and trusted too quickly. Often feeling frustrated, Lauren usually bit her tongue and let them work out their problems, but this time was different from anything Jane had experienced in the past. The sudden change in Damian's behaviour towards Jane caused her to wonder what the reason was for the drastic change in their relationship. Damian's disinterest in Jane worried Lauren much.

"Jane, have you two talked at all?

"I've tried to talk to him, but he isn't interested in being at home with me long enough for us to talk, or he leaves whenever I bring up anything."

"You need to leave him. I know you love him, but he is not being loving to you by ignoring and leaving you. You deserve so much better and more. A man who can't wait to see you at the end of his day, one who tells you how much you are loved every day is what you deserve, Jane." Lauren's anger and disappointment surfaced as the shell of her best friend sat in front of her. "You look like you haven't slept in days, along with being absent from your friends. No one has heard from you in several days; that isn't like you. I'm worried about you. Damian makes you feel so much less than you truly are, and he can't see your value. He should be willing to talk and work things out, or at the very least, express what is bothering him in your relationship. You know communication is the glue to any relationship, and this is why I am saying to you that you need to let Damian go. I'm so sorry to hurt you, but I can't bear to see you so sad and upset. I love you."

Jane couldn't help but feel the frustration in Lauren's words, and they were hurtful. Jane felt like she had to defend Damian to her friends throughout her entire relationship, especially to Lauren. None of her friends agreed with her decision to date him and struggled with being supportive during their three-year bond. Maybe they were right all along. Perhaps she was desperate to be with someone, and she settled for an emotionally immature man, who, at times, was verbally abusive. Being with someone who was not supportive, caring, and would never contribute equally in a relationship often had people making poor decisions out of fear of being on their own. Did she settle? Was she afraid of being on her own? Was she looking for something in Damian that he wasn't capable of giving her? Maybe she was weak and desperate to be loved, or what she believed was the love Damian gave her. In a hoarse whisper and with her head in her hands, Jane asked Lauren,

"What am I going to do?" Feeling hopeless, Jane wondered, *what am I going to do?*

The friends talked for some time, shared more tears, and even a few laughs before they hugged goodbye.

"Thank you for talking to me, Lauren. I love you too." Jane said before they went back to their respective jobs.

"I'm always here for you, Jane. Always."

"I know," Jane said with a smile. "I'll call you later."

"Promise?" Lauren questioned.

"Promise." Then Jane picked up the box of tissues and walked towards the elevators. But she felt embarrassed as she went by the security desk and saw Justin sitting there. With a last-ditch attempt to wipe away any smeared mascara from around her eyes, Jane wanted to apologize to Justin and return the box of tissue.

"Hi, Justin. Sorry to bug you. I just wanted to say thank you for the tissue, and sorry I caused a scene."

"No apology needed, and you certainly didn't cause a scene. I didn't want to interrupt, but you seemed upset, and I wanted to try to help."

"Well, thank you. I didn't introduce myself; I'm Jane," she said and held out her hand.

"Justin... um sorry, you already knew that," he said as his face flushed from embarrassment. "It's nice to meet you." He shook Jane's hand.

Justin's hand felt warm. He was very tall, at least six feet with strong arms and broad shoulders. He had light-brown hair, was clean-shaven, and had a kind smile and dark eyes, which Jane found hard to read.

"Are you working today?" he asked.

Jane sighed and stated, "Yes. I should let you get back to your work, and I need to get back to the unit."

"It was nice to meet you, and I hope you have a better afternoon." Justin smiled.

"Thank you," was all Jane said, for she knew her mind was too distracted, and if she were to be honest, work was the last place she wanted to be. She needed to talk to Damian.

Jane's text message notification rang as she walked towards the elevators. Her heart skipped a beat with the glimmer of hope it might be from Damian. But it wasn't. Instead, it was from Gabriel.

Hi Jane. How are you?

It was a simple message, and she wondered why he would be asking her how she was. Gabriel was behaving like she wished Damian would. With that thought, Jane sent a text to Damian.

We need to talk. Please.

Several minutes passed, with her message unanswered. Jane's heart ached more each time she checked her phone with no reply. As the remainder of the afternoon slowly coasted by, thoughts of her life with Damian distracted Jane as she assisted the patients.

To Jane's relief, the rest of the workday finally came to an end and still no word from Damian. The elevators were busy as eager people left work. As she waited patiently, Jane overheard a woman say to another, "I hope he likes the surprise dinner."

"I can't believe this time tomorrow you will be engaged! He'll love the dinner you'll have waiting for him. Text me how it goes. I'm so excited for you both!" the young woman squealed as the two women stood in the group waiting for the elevator.

Jane envied the excitement the women felt and wondered if she would ever be that happy again. The thought of being engaged to someone who loves them so much they couldn't imagine living another day without them was something Jane longed to hear from Damian. However, Jane knew that was nothing more than a forlorn reverie. The laughter of the women shook Jane from her self-pitying daydream. I'm going to put the ring on the dessert and cross my fingers he says yes," the young woman excitedly said.

"Oh, great idea. Just make sure he doesn't choke on it or be ready to save him from choking." The other woman giggled.

"Ha ha ha, very funny," the other woman chimed.

Jane wondered if a dinner of Damian's favourites might entice him to stay home long enough for them to talk. Maybe there was some hope yet to fix whatever was wrong between them. With that thought in mind, Jane decided that was what she was going to do, make his favourite meal.

The front door opened; it was 7:14 p.m. Damian paused in surprise, which turned quickly into indifference as Jane stood in the living room with a beer in hand waiting for him.

"Hi," Jane hesitantly said while she walked towards Damian and tried to hug him, but he stepped off to the side and avoided her advance. "I made dinner and thought maybe we could talk." Uncertainty clouded over any sense of hope she had.

"Talk? Why would we talk?" Damian questioned, then took a mouthful of beer.

"I thought it would be nice to spend some time together and maybe talk about the tension between us lately," Jane replied hesitantly. She looked down to the floor, unable to look at Damian, for she felt his disinterest, and her heart sank.

Damian walked over to the kitchen table, where a delicious roast beef dinner awaited him. With his back to Jane, he picked up a piece of beef and ate it while he thought to himself. Talk. that was the last thing on his mind. Taking another piece of meat, he turned and saw what he considered a pitiful, weak woman who he couldn't stand to be around any longer. The two of them talking about fixing their problems wasn't going to fix anything; he wasn't interested in putting any effort into his relationship with Jane. The continuous struggle to be with her became an unwelcomed chore he was tired of maintaining. It was time to free himself from Jane's neediness and whining. Her text messages and voicemails were aggravating, and he grew weary of seeing them every day. She needed to piss off and leave him alone. The very sight of her made him sick, and it was time he looked after himself and his needs, the primary one: to be free.

Chapter 4

"Oh my god, Jane. Are you ok?" Lauren's frantic voice yelled over the phone.

"He's gone," Jane said in nothing more than a whisper as tears streamed down her cheeks, and the lump in her throat made swallowing difficult. Although Jane heard Lauren speak to her, Jane couldn't comprehend anything she said. The deadness consumed her mind and body, leaving only emptiness in its wake.

"I'm coming over to get you!" Lauren exclaimed. But there was no response. "Jane? Jane? Did you hear me?" But again, nothing more than silence. Panic set in as Lauren grabbed her keys, slamming the door behind her, as thoughts of Jane's safety haunted her.

Jane let the phone fall to the pavement as weariness weighed heavily upon her about Damian. The night was all planned out with a delicious dinner and the two of them talking. She didn't understand what happened when everything went wrong. But Jane knew it was all her fault. If only she hadn't pushed Damian to talk, perhaps the evening would not have ended as it did. As Jane closed her eyes, her only thought was, how was she to manage with the essential part of her life gone? How was she to live without feeling his body against hers or tasting his kisses ever again? All their shared hopes dissipated into thin air in a matter of minutes. Her entire world shattered like glass, crippling Jane to her very soul. How was she supposed to forget Damian as though he never existed in her life? How was she supposed to stop loving him just because he stopped loving her? How would she get up every day knowing he wanted nothing to do with her, didn't love her anymore, and never wanted to see her again? How?

The extreme weight of her grief became too much to bear as her legs buckled beneath her, and she crumpled to the pavement trembling from the chilly night air, which blanketed her. The memories of their fight swarmed Jane's thoughts. "Damian, please don't leave me!" she begged. "I'm sorry for everything. Please, Damian. Just talk to me, please." The uncontrollable sobs heaved deeply from within her heart. Despite her pleas, nothing changed. Damian left in haste with Jane on his heels, desperately trying to salvage whatever she could of their relationship. But Damian had had enough, and things turned from bad to cruel for Jane.

"Life with you has been unbearable," he hissed with such venom it truly felt like he hated her. Before Jane had time to react, Damian turned, and suddenly Jane felt physical pain.

Hunched over, protecting herself, Jane felt a sharp sting to the side of her face before spinning around and falling to the floor. Jane couldn't comprehend what had just happened as she tried to regain the breath that got knocked out of her. The haziness Jane felt begun to subside enough for her to get back up onto her feet despite her body trembling. It was only then Jane realized what Damian had done to her. The tenderness which lingered confirmed he had hit her twice, despite the disbelief in her heart that he would physically hurt her. Jane couldn't just let Damian leave, but truthfully, she questioned if she was terrified of him leaving her or of being hit again. Damian had never done anything like that to her before. Did he hate her that much? Why?

Jane clumsily got up off the floor as her head spun and stumbled outside to Damian's truck. It was dark out, and the headlights blinded Jane even as she shielded her eyes. "Damian, please don't go. Don't leave me!" she sobbed. But it was useless; the truck backed out of the parking stall, the tires squealed, and he sped away. "Damian!" she cried out. "Please come back," Jane sobbed as she collapsed to the ground in a heart-wrenching meltdown.

Unaware of the time that had passed, Jane saw the moon and night sky masked in a cloud when she opened her eyes. She did not know if she had passed out from exhaustion or pain, which felt like a knife twisting deep inside her. The force with which Damian had punched her stomach and launched the backhanded blow to her face stunned Jane beyond words and made her heartbreak more sorrowful. The agony of hearing Damian's hostile-filled words about his feelings cut deep into her. In their wake, Jane felt the life of her soul evaporate while feelings of worthlessness and emptiness devoured her.

Jane lay in silence, churning over Damian's words. "I don't love you. You are pathetic. You are such a prude." The cruelty of his words felt just as painful as the physical abuse she sustained. The aftershocks of the pain initially clouded the memory of what he had done to her. Jane recalled how the second blow to her face knocked her to the ground, rendering her defenceless and helpless. Taking advantage of his opportunity, Damian had knelt beside Jane for a brief moment without saying anything as his eyes pierced hers. She recalled how scared she felt with his menacing presence hovering over her. In fear of being hit again, Jane had flinched, bringing her hands up to her face for protection. Damian laughed, relishing the power he'd held at that moment as he reached out and took hold of Jane's face, his fingers aggressively digging into her skin, ensuring his words would be heard and felt.

Fear radiated fiercely from her puffy, tear-filled eyes as he leaned in close and said, "You are nothing. You are a prude who never made me feel like a man. A man needs a woman, not a girl like you, Jane." His hand on her face tightened like a vice grip as he commanded her, "Look at me! I never loved you. You forced me to find another woman. Did you hear me, Jane? I've been fucking another woman who makes me feel more like a man than you ever did. You are nothing to me." Once the words left his lips, Damian paused a moment as though he suddenly regretted what he had done to her. In haste, Damian stood up, got his jacket, and went out to his truck without ever looking back, leaving the front door wide open.

The smell of rubber left behind by the tire marks on the pavement filled the air where Jane lay still. Feeling emotionally numb, Jane closed her eyes, giving no care to her safety or welfare. All of the hope she'd harboured and protected against any self-doubt about Damian's love disappeared as Jane lay in the parking lot. Feeling drained, Jane yeared to sleep and forget the whole night, but the pain in her abdomen worsened with a vengeance forcing Jane to stay present. She curled up in a fetal position and breathed in long, slow breaths to soothe the terrible pain. Jane needed to call Lauren; she needed help but couldn't gather the energy to call her, for the severity of the pain was too much.

A short time later, the pain subsided enough to focus on getting her cell phone from her back pocket and messaging Lauren.

Hey, can you come over? Damian and I fought, and things didn't go well. He hit me.

Jane knew Lauren would lose her mind, but she didn't know what else to do. One look at her face would give away what happened. There was no point in trying to hide it from her best friend. As Jane waited for Lauren to arrive, she soon realized how pathetic she must look lying on the ground, shivering from the chilly night air. Jane sat up and held a hand to her stomach for support. A few slow breaths helped Jane find her balance as she made her way back to the condo. A pensive feeling made her heart race with fear as she realized the front door was wide open. Was someone inside? Was Damian back, or was there possibly a stranger inside?

Jane paused before entering and called out, "Is anyone here?" It was silent as Jane pushed the door wide open and cautiously walked inside. The living room and kitchen area were just as she had left them, empty. Jane ensured the deadbolt was locked behind her, even though she knew if Damian wanted to get back in, he could do so with ease using his key. But deep down, Jane knew Damian was gone and wasn't coming back anytime soon. Shivers washed over her body; it was all too surreal to comprehend, and Jane curled up under a warm blanket on the sofa. The calm stillness and warmth soothed her worn and sore body. Despite the peacefulness, the unmistaken aroma of the roast beef dinner evoked memories of the evening's unforeseen events. The merciless and relentless ache was forever etched upon her heart and soul.

"I never loved you," echoed hauntingly in her mind, agonizing beyond anything Jane had ever experienced in her life. It was impossible not to feel the wrath of her heart's anguish as tears tumbled upon the blanket she held up close around her. "I'm leaving you. You are such a prude." Every word possessed her thoughts and felt cold, just like during their fight, with every spoken word filled with resentment towards her. Did he really hate her that much? Never before had he hurt her physically. Perhaps she pushed him too far, pushed him to resent and hate her and everything they had together. Was everything about their relationship a lie? Was anything real about his supposed love for her, or was that a cruel joke? Her entire world shattered in one fleeting moment, a passion built with a man whom she adored most ardently had been nothing but a lie for three years. Damian didn't love her, and he found another woman who made him feel like a man, someone who made him feel important and maybe even loved. The sting of his words filled her with heartbroken sorrow, and soon, Jane's sobs displaced the silence of the room.

"Jane?" a female voice yelled as fists frantically banged on the locked door. "Jane, let me in!"

The sound of the banging on the door startled Jane out of her numb state, making her heart stop at the thought Damian had returned. But to Jane's relief, it was Lauren. As she unravelled herself from the comfort of the blanket, it was as though the world spun in slow motion while she walked to the door.

"Jane, let me in!" Lauren yelled again.

Before Jane had an opportunity to say anything to Lauren, she barged through the door when it opened.

"Oh my god, Jane! What happened? Where is the asshole? Where is he!" she demanded. Lauren moved like a tornado, searching every room for Damian. After ensuring Jane was alone, Lauren noticed the bruising to the side of Jane's face and got some ice from the fridge. "That looks like it hurts," she said, gently holding some ice wrapped in a towel next to Jane's face.

But Jane remained quiet. The truth was, it did hurt, but no amount of physical pain could compare to the pain she felt deep within her core.

"Jane, I'm so sorry," Lauren said as she looked at Jane and saw not only the physical hurt but the sad, withdrawn look in her eyes. The sight of the bruising and split lip broke Lauren's heart. Jane was different, not just physically battered, but more so emotionally. The vibrant spirit that used to be so evident in her eyes and smile, which always sparked joy in others, was dimmed, almost lifeless. Lauren couldn't ever recall a time she saw Jane look so sad. Jane was kind, caring, and yes, naïve at times, but always a genuine heart who sacrificed time to help someone else before herself. Of all the people in Lauren's life, Jane least deserved to be treated so callously by a man who she was committed to and loved earnestly. What did Damian think he would gain from his behaviour? No matter how many excuses Lauren conjured up, the only logical one that came to mind was it had to be another woman. He must have found someone else and discarded Jane like a piece of trash. How dare he! Lauren's anger rose quickly, but one look at her devastated best friend, and she kept it under wraps.

There was no love lost between her and Damian. She never liked him from the first time they met; he was no good and not worthy of a woman like Jane. This night, more than ever, confirmed that firmly in Lauren's mind.

Unsure of what more to do for Jane, Lauren decided to talk about nothing important while tidying up the kitchen. But Jane barely heard a word she said as thoughts about the first time Lauren met Damian surfaced. What a disaster, she recalled. It was a double date with Lauren and her boyfriend. They all met for drinks at a local club where the music was too loud, making conversation nearly impossible to have. But Damian's attention was primarily on Jane, making conversation even more difficult and uneasy. He barely kept his hands off her and seemed to be completely unaware of how uncomfortable everyone was, or perhaps, he didn't care. Jane remembered how disappointed Damian was when she said they were going out and meeting some of her friends. For the first few months of their relationship, Jane decided it was time to introduce him to Lauren even though he never expressed any interest in meeting any of her friends and didn't offer to acquaint her with his. Despite her well-intentioned get-together, it turned out to be a less than stellar idea.

Lauren couldn't stand the awkward silence that plagued their conversation and tried to engage Damian; however, his manhandling of Jane frustrated Lauren. Jane remained polite despite her obvious embarrassment of Damian's continual assault upon her. Nonetheless, Lauren attempted to make conversation with him out of her love for her best friend. "Damian, Jane told me you work in construction."

All Damian could muster was an "Ah, huh" as he nibbled Jane's ear.

"You must work some long days and in all kinds of weather," was all Lauren cared to attempt, for Damian remained disinterested, with his focus only upon Jane. His inability to be social and act like a mature adult aggravated her beyond words. She couldn't wait for the night to be over.

Damian saw the look of frustration on Lauren's face, directed his attention away from Jane for a moment, and said, "I am a foreman on a site." Then he gulped his beer and stared unwaveringly at Lauren, in what seemed like a challenge to her to continue her interrogation of sorts.

Lauren didn't appreciate his challenging look; however, she decided to play his game out of mere curiosity to see where it would go. "What else do you like to do, Damian, besides groping Jane?" she said, as she took a sip of her wine and stared down Damian.

Jane gasped and then flushed with embarrassment. "Ok, you two, play nice," she said in a failed attempt to lighten the mood of that moment.

The night was a disaster with nothing more than forced conversation. It was all her fault, Jane believed. She should have just left things as they were instead of planning a night for everyone to meet.

But Lauren wasn't willing to let Damian get the best of her, and she provoked him more. "Damian, you certainly have occupied much of Jane's time. I barely see her anymore," Lauren said matter-of-factly.

"Jealous?" he said with a malicious grin as he ate some of his fries.

Lauren hated the sarcasm in his voice, but even more so, she despised his nefarious ego. "No, I'm not jealous, Damian, just curious."

"Oh. Curious about what?"

"Curious why you keep Jane away from her friends?" Lauren said as she leaned in closer to Damian.

"I don't keep her away from her friends. The real question is, why does she always choose me? Maybe we should ask her."

At that very moment, an abyss opened wide between the two people she loved most. Jane felt forced to mediate and cowardly turned away from their expectant stares with the belief she lacked the courage to stand up for herself and make them deal with their differences. Why would they make her choose between them? Did they not care about her enough to behave like adults and sort things out on their own? Why put her in a no-win position? Her head spun as her heart endured many emotions. *Ugh.* Jane didn't want to believe she always chose to spend her time with Damian, but when she thought back to how much time they spent together, maybe she did. The sudden realization that she had alienated herself from Lauren to be with Damian made her sick to her stomach.

"Well?" Damian impatiently demanded, interrupting Jane's thoughts.

Her mind raced to find a reasonable response to the dilemma she provoked by her past actions. She turned to face them both but could not meet their gazes and instead looked at the ground. "Damian, you are a special part of my life, and yes, I choose to be with you, but that doesn't mean there aren't other people who matter to me. I want everyone to get along so we can do things together." As soon as the words left her mouth, Jane shuddered with humiliation. They sounded so juvenile, even to her.

Damian laughed and mockingly looked at Jane, "Really? You want us all to get along so we can go out and play together? No, thanks. Let's get out of here." And he took Jane's hand in his. Damian turned to Lauren and said with smug sarcasm, "It's been great."

He gave Lauren shivers of the offensive kind. She peered over at Jane and saw a look of defeat on her pretty face. Clearly, she felt uncomfortable at being put in the middle of their egotistical strife. Guilt swept over Lauren; it wasn't fair of them to have put her in that position, and she decided at that moment, for the sake of her best friend's happiness, she would tolerate Damian. Rather than continue with the confrontation already started, Lauren wanted to go home and let things cool down between her and Damian. "Come on, let's all get out of here. I've got an early morning at work tomorrow." She gave Jane a big hug and whispered in her ear, "I'm sorry. I'll call you tomorrow." Lauren pulled away and saw her friend's eyes misted over with tears. Lauren couldn't help but feel guilty for her part in how the evening went. She should have been the bigger person, but Damian provoked something easily within her. It was a challenge, and she rarely backed away from them. Unlike the men Jane had introduced to her in the past, Damian was all kinds of wrong for her. Jane was utterly smitten with him, but deep down, Lauren knew he was bad news. Tonight's date, though, was not the right time to instigate a fight, and for that, she was sorry. To reassure Jane, Lauren reconfirmed, "We'll talk tomorrow."

Damian watched as the two friends shared a hug, and he silently enjoyed his win and Lauren's subsequent retreat. He smiled smugly as Lauren and her boyfriend, Steve, left, while he thought to himself, *She better watch herself; he wasn't going anywhere, and Jane was his.*

Lauren shivered despite the warm night. She knew he watched her as they all parted ways, and she thought to herself, *asshole.* Tonight would be one of a few times they would all get together, and that suited her just fine. Perhaps Damian would get bored of Jane after a while and leave her. Well, at least that was her hope, even though she knew Jane would be devastated. Lauren believed, though, it would be for her benefit in the end, and she would be there when that time came.

The two friends talked the next day to Jane's relief, and there were no hard feelings from Lauren towards her. But Lauren didn't hold back as she expressed her true feelings about Damian. "You can do so much better, Jane. You deserve to be loved and not forced to choose between your friends and your boyfriend. It's not right. I am worried about you."

"Damian loves me, and I enjoy spending time with him. So please, just be happy for me, and time will sort things out between you both. I know it will," Jane pleaded to Lauren.

Lauren, however, knew better. She knew Damian would never change. He was an asshole through and through, and no matter what Jane believed, time would not change anything between her and Damian. For the sake of her dear friend's fragile heart, Lauren decided to accept Damian was a part of Jane's life. "I promise you. I will support you and Damian. Our friendship means more to me, and I don't want to risk losing that. I love you, Jane."

"I love you too," Jane said with relief. "Thank you, Lauren."

Jane understood the reservations Lauren had towards Damian; however, she also knew where Damian was coming from. He had had a long day at work and just wanted to stay inside, order some food, get naked, and fuck till they could barely breathe. He had grown accustomed to being with Jane during the first few months of their relationship, enjoying their pure unadulterated lust for one another. She thought about him continually and wanted to spend every moment with him that she could. They did everything together, and Jane learned so much about herself. Despite what Lauren and others thought about Damian, he was the man who changed her life. He opened her heart to love and helped create the kind of intimacy Jane craved to share with a man. All the stories of romances and one-of-a-kind love were just fictional tales to her; that was until Damian entered her life. Jane daydreamed about his hands, his kisses, and of course, the way he made her body hum and come to life. Their appetite for one another was like a drug to her, and she couldn't get enough of him. His scent lingered on everything from bedsheets to the T-shirt of his she wore at night when he wasn't with her. Their relationship was dreamy and was everything to Jane. He was truly the love of her life.

But Lauren did know better, and her wish came true: Damian left her. Everything changed in one night; he went and took his love, leaving behind a shell of a woman, alone and broken. Despite their long-standing friendship, Lauren often was a bit insensitive and outspoken, usually when one didn't want to hear the black-and-white truth.

But Jane knew she would hear the dreaded words at some point, "I knew he was no good for you." The last thing, frankly, Jane wanted or needed to hear. Their mutual intolerance for one another made life challenging at times for Jane. She was very much aware of things around her but often chose to keep her thoughts to herself, despite usually being considered naïve by both of them. Unlike Lauren and Damian, who let their emotions or opinions be seen and heard, Jane was often silent and reserved, choosing to listen instead. But nothing matter anymore, Damian left her, and their relationship was over.

Jane pulled the blanket closer around her, thankful her friend was there with her now. She knew no matter what happened in her life, Lauren would show up for her. Someone who hated doing dishes cleaned every last one, and the kitchen, for her. Compelled to say something, Jane called out, "Lauren?"

"What's up, sweetie? What can I get you?" Lauren asked as she walked over to the sofa with a dishtowel in hand.

"Thank you," Jane said with tears trickling down her cheeks. "I'm sorry."

Without saying a word, Lauren sat beside Jane and hugged her tightly as she cried.

The two sat for a while in stillness, but Jane's mind was far from silent. She knew Lauren wanted to know what happened, but the constant churning of Damian's words was all she could think about, and honestly, Jane lacked the energy to relive everything that happened. He thought she was weak, a prude, and dreary, all the things he couldn't stand anymore, let alone love. The fact that she wasn't worthy of his love anymore was all that came to mind when she closed her eyes.

Lauren knew Jane couldn't stay at the condo and said, "Why don't you come and stay with me for a while, till you've sorted things out, then I know you'll be safe."

Jane nodded and stood up from the sofa, folding the blanket while she contemplated her next move. Lauren was right; she would feel safer if she stayed with her. Perhaps after some time, Jane wouldn't be as scared to be on her own.

"Ok, I'll pack some things." Jane didn't want to keep Lauren waiting long, as she grabbed clothes from the dresser while tears blurred her vision. In a daze, Jane walked to the closet where she saw Damian's clothes hanging. Tenderly she touched the sleeve of one of his leather jackets, recalling a time he wore it while they were out. It was on a date where he took her to dinner, and then they drove up the coast on his motorcycle in the moon's bright light. It was a fond memory of early in their relationship, one Jane treasured. She couldn't stop the flow of tears and sobbed while she packed a suitcase. All of the memories and his scent on his clothing felt like another punch to her stomach. It was all too much to handle. She crumbled onto the bed with a shattered heart and crushed soul. How was she going to manage without him in her life? How was she just to stop loving him? Too many unanswered questions to even know where to begin.

"Jane?" Lauren said as she softly knocked on the bedroom door. She heard Jane crying and hesitated before she knocked, wondering what she would say. Still unsure, Lauren opened the door and saw her friend sobbing on the bed; her own heart broke seeing Jane so distraught and overcome with grief. Never in all their years of being friends had she seen Jane like this. Unsure of what to say, she decided no words were needed and just hugged her instead.

A short time later, the two friends had Jane packed and ready to leave. Jane went through the apartment and turned off the lights while Lauren took the suitcases to her car. Just before she was about to turn off the last light, Jane froze in her tracks inside the front doorway. A long, slow breath left her chest as she looked about the apartment one last time. She'd called it home for three years and had created so many memories with Damian. Now, the apartment was cold, dark, and lifeless. Maybe it was all a lie from the very beginning. All of the chapters of their story were nothing but fiction. Perhaps she was naïve and foolish to believe she was capable of being someone Damian wanted to be with, to love, forever. But forever was a myth, only reserved for those timeless stories of great love often lost and then found. It belonged to those genuinely gifted with a fictional, forever-precious love such as Elizabeth Taylor and Richard Burton had or only in the movies like Allie and Noah. And although every relationship, whether fictional or not, experienced its hardships, Jane wondered why she and Damian couldn't weather theirs.

Why did everything have to end without any possibility of a happily ever after? Or maybe happily ever after was non-existent as well. Jane could feel the tears swell in her eyes again; she needed to leave despite her heart's purest desire. Out of sheer will and a need for self-preservation, with one click of the switch, the light disappeared along with everything Jane believed to be her home. She closed and locked the door, and at that moment, it became glaringly apparent to her that the story of Jane and Damian had come to an end.

As Lauren drove, Jane blankly stared out the window, completely unaware of anything around her. All that changed when she heard the notification on her cell chime. "Damian! It must be him!" she frantically scoured her purse for her cell.

Lauren let out a deep sigh and hoped it wasn't him as she watched Jane's hands shake while she read the text message.

The message read,

Hey, Jane. I just wanted to say hi and see how you are?"

She wasn't sure if she was seeing things due to her blurry vision from crying so much or from being exhausted when she realized who messaged her. Immediately upon seeing who it was, Jane stopped shaking; it was from Gabriel Lockhart.

"Was it Damian?" Lauren curiously asked.

Jane shoved the phone back in her purse, then replied, "No, it was someone from work. I'll message them back later." The truth was, she felt conflicted. Desperately so, Jane wished it was Damian telling her to come back, and he was sorry for everything. But instead, it was a man whom she felt safe around, but she couldn't disclose that thought to Lauren out of fear of judgment and her friendship with Brooke. It was just best not to say anything, and she lied to her best friend instead.

Chapter 5

Four days, ninety-six hours, 5,760 minutes had slowly and agonizingly passed since Damian said he didn't love her anymore and left. She was alone with no place to call home and no Damian. Jane stood in front of the bathroom vanity, where she starred absently into the mirror, feeling empty and lost as she listened to the soothing sounds of a warm shower running in the background. The woman who starred back with puffy eyes rimmed in black circles, a bruised cheek, and a split lip, was nothing more than a stranger. She was once happy and loved, but her hollow, sad eyes only saw the trauma left behind by someone she once trusted with her life. The physical pain paled in comparison to the unbearable ache in her soul. The despair unleashed recollections of Damian inflicting pain with not only his hands but with his words, which habituated her serially like a torturous horror movie. Every night her nightmares were haunted by Damian's hate-filled eyes burrowing through her as his venomous words ate away at her soul until she was merely a shell of her former self.

"Jane, sweetie, please come out. Why don't you have a shower or bath? It might help to make you feel a little bit better," Lauren said through the closed bedroom door. But Jane didn't reply, remaining in bed with the curtains drawn closed, not ready to face the world yet. A world without Damian, a world on her own.

Given how much time had passed, Jane decided she probably should force herself out of bed and shower. Jane dreaded every moment she was awake and found it hard not to question what she was going to do. Not having Damian be a part of her every day spawned thoughts of guilt that she didn't do enough to save their love. The suffocating blame Damian expressed of Jane not being enough of a woman for him consumed her. Maybe she didn't show him love the way he desired or needed, or perhaps she was weak, and he needed the kind of love she was incapable of giving. Whatever led to their demise destroyed what little self-worth Jane had, leaving behind a fractured shell of a woman who didn't know who she was on her own.

Damian was her first real love; Jane never honestly had the love of a man before, and it was the most beautiful thing. Waking up every day with him made her happy, and knowing he chose her made Jane feel cherished. Together they had someone to share every day with and had hopes and dreams of building a life together. That was Jane's happiness; Damian was her happiness. Maybe it was wrong to value a person's feelings for her and their presence in her life more than believing those same things about herself. Perhaps it was her programming about love and the worth it had in her life. She was like most people who let their past experiences notably affect their present ones. As all these thoughts swirled about her compartmentalized mind, Jane couldn't help but feel empty despite the inner wisdom perilously trying to surface from her heart.

Emotionally vulnerable with a mind full of what-ifs and how-comes of her recent breakup with Damian, Jane's thoughts wandered to the troublesome relationships of her past. Patterns start somewhere, and Jane's began with Cory, her first boyfriend in university. Although their connection was brief, it commenced the self-destructive landslide of her self-worth when it was in its infancy. He left her for one of the most popular sorority girls on campus. She determined that they were both young and convinced herself he wasn't her forever love, and she eventually found a way to move on. Then there was Shawn, a porter at the hospital where Jane got her first job as a graduate nurse. They enjoyed almost two years together, and she was head over heels in love with him. He earned a fantastic opportunity to go to an elite school across the country, and he couldn't pass it up. They cared deeply for one another and chose to work through their long-distance relationship together and not to break up. Early on, they saw one another every few weeks, but their busy lives with school and shift work, and the cost of travelling, challenged their love.

After about six months, Jane watched her friends with their boyfriends, and she felt the weight of her loneliness. Their long-distance love edged closer every day to becoming a distant memory, so Jane planned a surprise visit one weekend in the hopes of reigniting that spark once again. But the surprise was entirely on her. She knocked on the door of his apartment, only to be greeted by an attractive woman dressed in one of Shawn's business shirts with tousled, just-fucked hair. Jane stood frozen, unable to speak. Shawn stepped out into the hallway, wrapped in only a towel, saying how sorry he was and wished she hadn't found out like this. It was hard for Jane to forget the humiliation she felt at that moment, but she knew she never wanted to feel that kind of humiliation again.

Experiencing the physical pain Damian had inflicted upon her was something Jane had never experienced before at the hands of another human being. The worst part wasn't the actual physical pain. It was the psychological warfare that ravaged her when she was awake and when she slept. The negative self-talk and the limiting beliefs that she didn't do enough to make the relationship work preyed upon Jane heavily. Despite all her past humiliations, nothing prepared Jane to hear Damian's vicious and callous words. Did it mean Jane made it all up in her head that he loved her and wanted a shared life together? Was she so desperate to be loved, she believed whatever Damian said or did was love for her? God, she was pathetic and naïve! It made her sick to her stomach.

The never-ending flood of negative and devaluing self-talk plagued Jane, and the worst part of it all, she believed it. Her world flipped upside down; she lost everything that meant anything to her. Mixed among the hurtful things Jane told herself was the thought that if she were smarter or more aware, perhaps she would have been able to see their relationship for the scam it was and save herself the heartache and betrayal. Jane loved Damian. No matter what anyone said to her about his ego or his less than desirable behaviour, she wouldn't have listened to them. Even her best friend, Lauren, expressed her dislike of Damian from the beginning, and she could do better. But Jane dismissed everyone else's opinion except her own. Maybe it was true: love is blind. Damian was her forever love.

Jane's mind wandered to a time early on in their relationship when Damian wanted her. They made love or had quickies every day. She loved so many things about Damian, but there was one, in particular, she kept secret, even from Lauren. Even if Jane had told Lauren, she probably wouldn't have believed her. He was very dominant when they were intimate. Initially, it frightened Jane, but over time, she found her way and enjoyed how they were together when he made love to her or when they savagely fucked one another.

One morning, Damian came up behind Jane as she was getting dressed for work. "Hey baby, I need you." He slid his hands across her ass cheeks, slowly kneading them.

There were no more words exchanged, only a hungry, hedonistic heat between them. Damian weaved his hand into her hair, pulling it forcefully to the side. His fingers trailed down her throat, creating a wave of goosebumps across her skin, much to his delight. Her breath was shallow and fast as he slowly made his way to her ample cleavage, tracing it with the tip of his finger. All the while, she held her breath in anticipation of his exquisite torment.

In his hands, Jane's sultriness hid her vulnerability, but, with one touch from Damian, her wanton inner slut was set free from its gilded cage. She felt heavenly, and he wanted more. He needed more. The softness of her skin enticed his hand, and he cupped the fullness of a breast while he pulled her head back further and massaged her.

"You have a fucking rocking body!" he growled in her ear. "And I'm going to enjoy it in any way I want," he said as he roughly pulled her head back, asserting his dominance over her.

Jane's eyes dilated as hedonistic lust radiated from her body. She parted her lips, then gave a come-hither smile. She was captivating in every way. Damian needed no further encouragement to devour her. His lips roughly captured Jane's full pink lips, their tongues savouring one another, fueling their mutual hunger for more. Pulling away from their kiss with his hand still fisted in her hair, Damian pushed her down to her knees. Jane's eyes opened, and a devious smile crossed her lips as he freed his rigid cock from its denim confines, for his need grew insatiably seeing Jane kneeling in front of him. Jane tauntingly gazed into Damian's eyes with a mischievous grin and slowly licked her lips with anticipation at the sight of his pre-cum glistening in the light. The tip of her tongue twirled around and around the head of his cock, lapping up the sweetness.

"Mmm," Jane moaned with salacious hunger as her lips enveloped him almost entirely, guiding him deep within her throat.

Damian moaned as ecstasy consumed him. "Ah, fuck me." His hand fisted her hair tightly, making Jane whimper, but Damian didn't care, for the velvety wet warmth of her mouth made all of his cares and stress disappear. He felt his knees quiver, and he grabbed hold of the dresser as Jane had him teetering on the edge of euphoria. With only a few more strokes of her lavish tongue, she would bring him to his knees. "Yes! Faster. Harder," he demanded, guiding the speed with his hand, fucking her mouth.

With every forceful thrust deep within her throat, Jane thought she would throw up and tried her best not to gag so much. Hearing the pleasure in his moans and knowing he was close to cumming made Jane want to please Damian more than ever.

"Ahhh, don't stop," Damian panted. He could barely stand and leaned against the dresser, holding on with both hands while he watched Jane suck and stroke him with fervour and need. Damian held his breath as he felt his engorged scrotum release and ejaculate race up his stiffened shaft, giving him a mind-blowing orgasm. He gripped the dresser, letting out a feral howl loud enough for the neighbours to hear. His body shook uncontrollably as Jane's mouth filled with his warm cum and seeped from her lips down her chin, coming to its final resting place upon her vivacious chest. "Ahhh," growled Damian one last time as his body experienced aftershocks from the climax.

Jane remained on her knees as she relished the salty creaminess that coated the back of her throat and tongue. Jane knew how turned on he would be if she were to seductively place her cum-coated fingers, one at a time, in between her lips and alluringly lick her fingers clean. Once done, she held out her hand and waited for Damian to help her to her feet.

"That was amazing!" Damian exclaimed.

Jane's heart swooned. She enjoyed hearing him cum, knowing she did that to him; there simply was nothing better to her. Feeling his hand fisted in her hair made her feel calm as opposed to scared. She wasn't sure exactly why, but kneeling before him felt safe. Jane relished Damian's dominance.

As Jane saw her reflection looking back at her, she realized those intimate moments she used to have with him, feeling safe and loved, were gone. Instead, her days were plagued with a sabotaging war between her heart and her head. Jane needed to silence the crippling voices with a warm, consoling shower and soon submerged herself under the stream of warm water. With eyes closed, Jane relished the feeling of the cascading water raining down upon her, secretly hoping it would cleanse away her guilt and shame and ease her mind. Its heavenly warmth lifted some of the burdensome weight from her neck and shoulders as the water rained down. A wave of nausea washed over Jane, and she steadied herself against the shower wall, bracing herself as her knees felt as though they would buckle beneath her. She was unsure if the heat from the water or the exhaustion made her feel so unwell. It seemed the escape from her sorrow was fleeting. Her overwhelming worries of no home to go to, no purpose, and no one to love, had Jane wondering if she would ever feel whole again instead of being fragile and incomplete. It was too much to handle being continually beaten up by the harsh guilt she always felt. Questions of could she have done more; should she have done more, then maybe Damian would have stayed, echoed in her every thought. It was impossible to escape them and the shame, both of which weighed upon her exhausted body. Unable to escape it all, Jane sat in the tub, hugging her knees with the warm water falling upon her.

"Ahhh," Jane cried out as cold water fell upon her like shards of ice. Quickly, she reached for the tap and shut off the water. Jane lost track of time while trapped in her thoughts about everything and anything about her life. Her skin pebbled with goosebumps, and she reached for a towel, but there wasn't one close at hand. "Damn," she cursed quietly to herself as she realized she had forgotten to put the towel on the rack. Awkwardly, Jane shivered as she reached for the towel on the vanity as another wave of nausea hit her. The all-too-familiar stabbing pain deep within her abdomen was more intense this time and took her breath away.

"Ooooh," Jane said out loud as she slumped to the floor with a thud, guarding her abdomen with a hand.

"Jane? Jane? Are you ok?"

She heard footsteps running down the hallway towards the bathroom.

Jane barely caught her breath before the forceful knocking on the door began with Lauren's frantic voice on the other side, calling out to her. *The pain is worse than before*, Jane thought to herself before saying, "I'm... I'm fine. Sorry I worried you. I slipped, but I'm ok."

"You don't sound fine, Jane," Lauren questioned through the closed door.

God love her friend. Lauren had a flare for drama, but Jane knew Lauren was only concerned for her and the tragedy she couldn't seem to escape as of late. Jane loved Lauren for her unwavering friendship, knowing she would always be there for her. But every friendship and relationship had boundaries, possibly even an expiry date of sorts. Jane was afraid of losing Lauren if she wasn't careful. Truthfully, she wasn't okay, but Jane saw no other option. Being weak and needy made her lose Damian. She couldn't risk losing Lauren as well. Jane slowly stood up, taking a deep breath in. She held onto the vanity as the stabbing pain subsided once again. Once on her feet, Jane looked in the mirror. *You do this, Jane.* She put a smile on her face and opened the door before Lauren tried to break it down with her forceful knocks.

"See? I'm good," Jane said, hopeful her reassurance was enough for Lauren to see she was, in fact, ok. Well, at that moment, anyway. She had helped her so much over the last few days, and she knew Lauren was genuinely concerned about her. Guilt overcame Jane as she said, "I'm so sorry I startled you."

"I was worried," Lauren said, and the concern on her face softened when she saw for herself Jane was all right.

"You know I'm a klutz." Jane smiled goofily and hugged her friend.

"Argh, you're all wet!" Lauren frowned but hugged Jane back despite being soaked.

Jane looked at her friend and knew Lauren's unquestionable allegiance to their friendship was unconditional, without a doubt, and she would always be there for her. Lauren was her family, and that meant everything to Jane. Gratitude filled Jane's heart, and all she could think to say was, "thank you," as she gave Lauren a hug and a kiss on her cheek.

Lauren nodded as she tried to swallow away the lump in her throat as she hugged Jane back.

"Are you off to work soon?" Jane asked.

"I can work from home today if you would like to hang out?" she offered.

"No, you go to work. I'm good. Was thinking of looking at the rental ads for a place to live," Jane said.

"Why don't you just live here for a while and see what happens?" Lauren asked.

"Lauren, Damian, and I are over; I know that. There has been nothing from him since the night we broke up. It's clear we're over. And to be honest, I couldn't be alone with him again, even if he wanted me back. Things are very different now." As she heard her own words, goosebumps blanketed Jane's skin, and a flashback of Damian's anger made her shudder.

Lauren saw the fear in Jane's crystal blue eyes as she brought up Damian's name. Rather than push the subject, she chose instead to say with a kind smile, "Ok. I'll see you tonight, and we can order in."

Relieved, Jane replied, "Sounds good. Have a good day. Oh, and make sure you change." She giggled at the sight of Lauren's wet clothing.

"Bitch." Lauren teased.

"You love me, and you know it," Jane countered back with a smile.

"You know it!" Lauren exclaimed as she walked down the hall into her room.

The day flew by, leaving Jane to feel like she hadn't accomplished a whole lot. After a walk to clear her head, she began to wonder about where she would live. Would she be able to afford a place on her own? Working a couple of extra shifts each month or possibly finding a roommate were the only options Jane could think of doing, but neither one thrilled her. She already worked an extra shift a month, and the idea of a stranger living with her made Jane feel anxious. These felt like discouraging tasks. Every apartment for rent was too expensive, too far away, or no bigger than a bachelor suite. Would she find a place to live she could call home again, or would she have to stay with Lauren and feel like an unwanted guest who wouldn't leave? All hope quickly diminished as she continued to look at the endless ads. Maybe it was best to stop for the day as her stomach reminded her it was close to dinner, and she hadn't eaten anything all day.

Jane texted Lauren.

Hey. What about Chinese tonight?

Sounds yummy. I'll pick it up on my way home. Say half an hour or so.

Great!

Jane looked at her phone message from Gabriel, which she didn't answer other than with a quick message saying she was home. The truth was he asked a loaded question, and these days Jane wasn't sure how she would tell others about her breakup with Damian. It was a bit too soon for her. The idea of telling people, especially Gabriel, about Damian leaving her and how she was homeless wasn't how Jane wanted to start conversations with everyone and embarrass herself. But, despite the guilt and shame, part of her wanted very much to tell Gabriel everything. She knew he would listen without judgment and make her feel safe; however, she also knew he would be upset about Damian hitting her and decided it was best not to disclose everything. It had been a few days since he texted her, and Jane felt guilty for not sending a proper reply sooner. It seemed to Jane she could no longer avoid Gabriel, and a part of her didn't want to.

Hi. Sorry it took a few days to get back to you. Damian and I broke up a few days ago. I am staying with Lauren for a while. I hope you are doing well. Thank you for saying hi.

It didn't take long for Gabriel to send a reply back to Jane.

I'm sorry to hear about you and Damian. It is good you are staying with Lauren. How are you doing?

I'm tired, heartbroken. Damian told me he never loved me.

Tears misted her eyes, making it hard to see what her fingers texted back. It was nearly impossible not to get so emotional every time she recalled his words.

Gabriel texted back,

Would you like to meet for a coffee and talk?

Something within her screamed yes. Maybe it would help to be around someone who wouldn't judge her or make her feel naïve and small. Jane knew Lauren saw her as weak, and although Jane couldn't disagree with her, she also knew herself. She was allowed to grieve the loss of someone whom she loved more than anything. There were many moments during their relationship where his heart was open despite what he told her. She knew he did love her at one time, and over the last four days, Jane had explored her thoughts about why his love for her had died. She certainly wasn't the only person to blame, as every relationship takes both people to make it work or to let it die. There were many questions Jane had, but the only person who could answer them no longer spoke to her.

Jane decided to take the leap and meet him.

Coffee would be nice. I'm back to work tomorrow. Would around 5 p.m. work?

Great. Let's meet at The Coffee House near the hospital.

Ok, sounds good. I will text you if I am going to be a bit late getting off work. Otherwise, I'll see you then.

I look forward to seeing you, Jane.

Chapter 6

"Argh," Jane sighed as the alarm rang out, harshly reminding her she had to return to work this day. She yawned several times, feeling tired as she recalled the restless sleep. Jane rolled over, hoping she was just dreaming and it wasn't time to get up, but no such luck as 5:30 a.m. stared her in the face. "Time to get up," Jane said out loud to herself, but as she moved to sit up, a sharp pain in her abdomen took her breath away, causing her to lay back down till it seemed to subside on its own a few moments later. As it passed, Jane sat up, waiting to see if it would return.

Jane walked to the bathroom and took a couple of pain pills, hoping the ache would go away so she could get on with her day. Much to her dismay, the familiar abdomen pain returned with a vengeance as Jane got ready for work. Slow, deep breathing seemed to reduce it to a tolerable dull ache, but something definitely seemed off to Jane. Today, she would see one of the doctors at work.

Driving to work, Jane hoped the distraction of the workday would allow her mind a brief timeout of the thoughts from the last few weeks. One thing was sure; she had no intention of focusing on everything she had recently lost. Instead, she was going to start this day new. But despite her noble intentions, many cumbersome thoughts continued to plague her, no matter how hard she tried to silence them. Jane couldn't help but think of Damian. How was he doing? Was he staying at the apartment? Did he miss her at all? She realized at that moment, though, that to move forward, she had to release her attachment to Damian. Not surprisingly, there was no communication from him since their last encounter. But something she didn't think about was perhaps the pain she had been experiencing was related to the trauma from Damian's aggression. A shaky breath escaped her lips as a memory from that evening crept back to her consciousness. Expelling a long, slow breath, Jane realized how thankful she was to be going to work, and she would soon be seeing all the familiar faces, which she missed.

Jane walked through the sliding glass doors of the hospital, and a feeling of coming home crept up on her. Most people would think she was crazy, but Jane did enjoy her nursing job. She had graduated as one of the top few of her class and felt she had found her purpose, her calling. The day she was hired at San Fransisco General was one of the best things to ever happen to her, and just like that day, the sun's rays filled the vast lobby through all of the windows, blanketing everyone with its warmth. The sun's heat felt like bliss upon Jane's face as she looked up to the vibrant blue heaven and felt a sense of calm wash over her body and mind. Even for those brief few minutes in time, Jane relished the quietness within her. It felt so good to be back, she quietly thought to herself.

"Excuse me," a woman's voice said behind Jane.

Jane turned around to find an older woman with a kind smile and a look of confusion in her eyes. "Do you need some help?" Jane asked politely, thankful for the distraction.

"I seem to be lost. Are those the elevators that would take me to unit 42?" the stately woman asked.

"They are. I am going to the same floor, and I can show you to the unit if you like," Jane offered.

"You are very kind, thank you." The woman smiled.

Jane smiled back, and the two women walked towards the elevators chatting with one another. They passed by the security desk, where a few people stood talking to the guards; the hospital seemed to be busier than usual, Jane noticed quietly to herself. Justin, the security guard, smiled at her as she walked by but could not do his usual banter with her as he was chatting with a couple. Jane had to admit, with a sense of relief, she welcomed the fact Justin couldn't hassle her about her absence from work. The idea of telling people about her break up with Damian depressed her.

"Thank you for helping me," the older lady said upon seeing the elevators.

"You're welcome," Jane said. Jane was about to push the button to the elevator when she heard a familiar voice call out to her.

"Hey, Jane! Wait up," the male voice said.

"Sigh, no such luck," Jane whispered to herself before turning to see Justin walking towards her.

"How are you doing? Haven't seen you at work the last few days," he asked.

And there it was: the question Jane dreaded to the very depth of her soul, and no doubt would be asked many more times throughout the day. "Hi, Justin. I'm ok," Jane began to answer, but then, suddenly, the world started to spin, and a wave of nausea washed over her as the all-too-familiar stabbing abdominal pain returned with a vengeance at that moment. It was worse than anything she had previously felt before, taking her breath away. Jane hunched over as her pain felt like a thousand knives stabbing into her. Something was terribly wrong, and she needed help. "Justin, I don't..." and that was all Jane said before the world went black.

Justin noticed Jane's ghostly pale complexion as her eyes rolled back and her body went limp, collapsing to the floor. "Jane!" Justin yelled as he ran to her side, shocked and fearful at the sight of her lifeless body lying in the middle of the lobby. He called out her name again, "Jane, wake up!" Frantically, Justin called for help on the radio as some other hospital staff ran towards them to help identify her as one of their own.

"Here is a wheelchair," a man dressed in a security guard uniform said. I'll take her to emergency.

"Let's lift her on three. One, two, three," Justin called out. With ease, both men carried Jane to the chair.

Justin saw another security person run towards them. "Call the ER and tell them we are coming with a woman who collapsed and won't wake up."

The guard nodded and ran to the desk to make the call.

The two men ran down the hall towards the emergency area. As Justin looked at Jane, he couldn't help but feel extremely worried. She didn't look good at all. The colour completely drained from her pretty face while her hands went ice cold.

"Jane Riley, please can you tell me where she is?" Lauren demanded of the emergency desk nurse.

"Are you any relation to the patient?" the woman asked politely.

"I'm her best friend and her emergency contact. I received a call she was here. She doesn't have any family. Please, I need to know where she is," Lauren frantically expressed to the triage nurse. She was so worried about Jane. All the hospital social worker told her was that her best friend collapsed as she was going to work. Lauren knew Jane wasn't feeling well this morning, despite her telling Lauren she was ok to go to work. The loud bang in the bathroom drew Lauren's attention that there was a problem, but she also knew Jane would put on a brave face and do her best to push through whatever was making Jane unwell. Lauren saw how pale Jane looked when they talked in the kitchen over morning coffee, but she kept it to herself to not start an argument. Jane had enough stress on her mind.

The triage nurse paused a moment, then said, "She is in surgery. Go to the fourth floor, and you will see the nurse's desk to find out more about your friend."

"Thank you!" Lauren stated as she turned and ran down the hall to the elevators. Surgery! Why? Lauren questioned as worry took over. She had to find Jane.

"Please, please, you've got to tell me what is happening with my friend Jane Riley!" Lauren frantically exclaimed to the nurse on the fourth floor. "Please." Tears flooded Lauren's hazel eyes as she waited for the nurse to say something to her.

"What is the patient's name, Miss?"

"Jane Riley. I was told she was in surgery. I'm her emergency contact. Please, you have to tell me how she is!"

"What is your name, Miss?" the polite nurse asked in a soft but controlled tone.

"Lauren Taylor."

"I'll page the nurse assigned to help your friend. She'll come see you," she said.

A few minutes later, another nurse came and introduced herself and suggested they sit in the waiting area.

"I understand you are Jane's friend. I'm very sorry to say that Jane had an ectopic pregnancy which ruptured today. She lost a lot of blood and needed emergency surgery."

"Oh my god!" Lauren cried out. "Do you know how long she will be in surgery? Is she going to live?" She gasped at the thought of Jane dying as tears streamed down her face.

The nurse saw how distraught Lauren was and felt terrible being the bearer of the unsettling news about her friend. "No, unfortunately. I suggest you wait here, and I will let the doctor know you are here so he can update you on how things are going. Here's some tissue for you," she kindly offered.

Lauren couldn't speak and nodded as she took a seat in the waiting room. How could this happen? Her best friend may die, she thought to herself, feeling everything happening to Jane was all too surreal. What was she going to do? Lauren sat going over everyone Jane knew so they could be updated. But as Lauren wondered who to tell, she came up with only one name: Damian.

Should she text him or not? *Fuck! What should I do? It was his baby; he should know just how much he fucked up and abandoned her to deal with it on her own. What an asshole!*

Lauren texted,

Thought you should know Jane is in surgery right now. She had an ectopic pregnancy rupture and lost a lot of blood. Jane is at San Fran Memorial.

She hoped her words made sense as she typed through her teary, blurred vision. Lauren didn't know if he would reply or not, but at least he knew. The idea of Jane being pregnant with his child made her sick to her stomach. Lauren didn't believe he had been in touch with Jane since he left her, but maybe knowing he could have been a father may get him to see her or, at the very least, message her back. In the meantime, Lauren paced the hallway, hoping to distract herself from her best friend's unknown future.

A couple of hours had passed before the surgeon walked into the waiting room and saw a young lady about Jane's age sitting alone with her face streaked with tear-smeared mascara. "You must be here for Jane," he asked quietly, in hopes of not startling her. But the woman continued to stare blankly at the floor, lost in her thoughts. "Miss, are you family of Jane Riley?" the doctor asked.

"No, I'm her best friend," Lauren said with urgency as she recognized that the man standing in front of her was a doctor.

"I'm sorry, I can only speak to family, Miss," the surgeon said and turned to leave.

"Oh, wait! Please. I am also her emergency contact. She doesn't have any family. Please, you must tell me how she is!" Lauren pleaded.

The surgeon turned, extended his hand, and kindly smiled. "My name is Dr. Thomas. I have been with Jane since she came into the emergency."

"What happened to her?" Lauren asked, relieved he was talking to her.

"Please, let's sit for a moment," Dr. Thomas said.

Immediately, Lauren's heart stopped as her mind prepared for what she feared would be news she was not prepared to hear. Jane was dead. *Oh god!* she silently screamed to herself.

The surgeon saw Lauren's eyes filled with uncertainty. "It's ok. Jane is doing fine and is in recovery. You can ease your mind," the doctor said with a calmness in his voice. "The surgery went well, and she will remain in the recovery room for a while yet before you can see her." Immediately, Lauren's grief-stricken panic released its hold upon her, and Lauren wept as relief filled her heart and mind.

"I'm sorry," Lauren apologized, embarrassed by her emotional state.

The doctor let her have a moment to collect herself, then said, "Jane collapsed in the lobby of the hospital. I understand she works here as a nurse."

Lauren, too impatient, had to ask, "What happened?"

"There is often significant blood loss from a ruptured ectopic pregnancy, resulting in a patient experiencing a loss of consciousness. She was brought to the emergency by staff, and we were able to get the bleeding under control and removed the damaged tissue of her right ovary and fallopian tube. She will remain in the recovery room for the next hour or so. Afterward, she will be transferred to unit 40, and you can see her there."

"I have to wait to see her still?" Lauren couldn't wait any longer; she needed to know if Jane was really going to be ok. "She will live, right? There won't be any complications?"

"She lost a lot of blood, and the more immediate concern is any sign of infection, but she will be watched closely. We have no reason to believe she won't make a full recovery.

Although Lauren heard his words, she wasn't sure if it was the surreal feeling of almost losing her best friend, but she found it incredibly hard to focus on the surgeon's words. As her mind caught up with the reality of the situation, Lauren gasped out loud and covered her mouth with her hands in her realization. *Jane was pregnant! Oh my god! Did she know? If she did, why wouldn't Jane have told her? Maybe she didn't know.*

The thought of her best friend unconscious from surgery after almost dying caused Lauren to hyperventilate and feel her chest tighten slightly. She looked for the glass of water given to her by a nurse while she waited. But when she looked down, Lauren paused briefly at the sight of her trembling hands. Lauren didn't understand initially but soon realized, for the first time in her life, she was terrified.

"Lauren!" she heard the voice of her fiancé say and was soon wrapped in his arms. Never before this moment had he ever seen Lauren so upset or felt her tremble. She was terrified of losing Jane, and instantly, his heart broke for her. He always saw Lauren as strong, independent, and a rebel at problem-solving, but this time, she couldn't fix it.

"Thank you, Doctor," Lauren said. He nodded and disappeared behind the restricted area doors.

"She needs to be ok. She can't die." Lauren sobbed into her fiancé, Steve's, shoulder. "I'm so happy you're here. Thank you."

Unsure of what to say, he decided against saying anything at all; instead, he just held her tightly in his safe arms. All they could do now was wait and see how Jane recovered.

Jane heard voices, but everything seemed like a dream full of muffled voices. She was unable to open her eyes or move her body. Unable to call out for help, unable to feel anything, and unsure of where she was. Paralyzed. It freaked her out. Even the voices didn't sound familiar to her, nor could Jane make out what they said. All Jane felt was extremely tired and decided to give in to the calm of her desire to sleep.

"Miss Riley?" a woman's voice gently called out. "It's time to wake up."

Jane heard the woman's voice again, but it wasn't real. She was asleep, and she was dreaming.

"Jane, you need to open your eyes," the woman insistently said.

Jane began to stir and slowly tried with all her might to move, but her body wouldn't, or couldn't. It felt like an invisible weight was laid down upon her, making it impossible to move. She desperately wanted to move, but all she could do was slowly open her eyes. Jane felt like she had the worst hangover of her life. But she was confused. There was no way she was drunk. Jane was sure of it, but why did she feel so out of it and unable to move? Her mind panicked. *Why can't I move? What happened to me?* She needed help. "Help me!" she tried to say, but her voice was silent. And soon, she drifted off to sleep once again.

"Jane? I'm here," another woman's voice said.

Jane opened her eyes in response to the voice she swore she heard, but her vision was blurred, and the room spun. It sounded like Lauren's. But why would Lauren be with her? After a few minutes, Jane's vision cleared slightly, and the room stopped spinning so she could see Lauren sitting next to her holding her hand.

"Thank God, Jane. You're ok." Lauren bowed her head into her hands in relief. When she looked back up to Jane, there was confusion upon her pale face.

Jane desperately tried to focus her eyesight so she may see her best friend. But to Jane's shock and disorientation, Lauren looked terrible, as though she hadn't slept in days. Her eyes were puffy and rimmed with smudged mascara, entirely out of the norm for Lauren. *What is wrong with her? Why is she so upset? What happened?*

"Why are you here?" Jane mumbled softly and tried to clear her throat. Her mouth was so dry it made speaking a challenge. Again, Jane softly spoke, "Why do you look so bad?"

Lauren suddenly laughed and squeezed Jane's hand. "I'm so relieved and thankful you are ok," she exclaimed as she stood up and decided she needed to hug her instead. She couldn't get Jane close enough.

"Agh!" Jane cried out. Her abdomen was so sore, but why?

"Oh my god, Jane, I'm so sorry. I didn't mean to hurt you," she said with tears misting over her eyes. "Jane, I have something to tell you."

The pain mainly subsided, leaving behind a dull ache. Jane was able to move her head and hands now for some reason. She no longer felt paralyzed, although she still didn't understand what was happening. The familiar sound of a monitor beep, the sound of the intravenous pump pushing fluid through the tube, and the site of a nurse nearby, had Jane wondering what had happened to her? Her eyes followed the tubing to where it ended, at her hand. She was in the hospital, but why? Her hand touched her face, and she discovered there was a nasal cannula inserted in her nose with oxygen flowing. "What happened? Why am I in the hospital?" Jane asked out loud.

"Jane, you are in the hospital. You had surgery," Lauren said quietly. "It's ok. You are all right now."

"Now? What happened, Lauren?" Jane said, alarmed by the word now. "Why am I in the hospital?" She tried to sit up, and, once again, the searing pain prevented her from doing so. "Why won't this pain go away?" she cried out.

"I'll go get a nurse. I'll be right back." Lauren said before she disappeared from the room. The truth was, Lauren didn't have the heart to tell Jane what had happened, that she was pregnant and lost the baby.

A moment later, a nurse returned with Lauren. "Good to see you awake, Miss Riley. How are you feeling?"

Still confused about everything, all Jane could think to ask was, "What happened?"

"You had surgery earlier today. I will get Dr. Thomas, and he can go over everything with you. In the meantime, try to rest and not move too much. Do you have any nausea?" the nurse asked.

"No," was all Jane replied. She looked to Lauren for answers. But the look on Lauren's face was not comforting to her. She was worried about something. "Lauren, why did I have surgery?"

Lauren wasn't sure what to tell Jane. She worried about whether or not she knew she was pregnant. "Jane, I don't know how to tell you this."

"Tell me what, Lauren?"

Lauren looked around the hospital room and let out a heavy sigh. She sat down on the bed beside Jane, took her hand, and gazed into her eyes. "Jane, you had surgery because you had a ruptured ectopic pregnancy. You passed out in the lobby of the hospital before you went to work. You needed emergency surgery to stop the bleeding. You would have died," Lauren paused as tears welled up in her eyes and tumbled down her cheeks. "I'm so sorry, Jane."

Jane heard every word Lauren said. But maybe it was the residual sedation drugs from the surgery in her body that made Lauren's words seem dreamlike, unreal. She could have sworn Lauren said she was pregnant. Jane's face wrinkled in confusion as she tried to put the pieces together from what she could remember. The sunlight had felt warm on her upturned face upon walking into the vast lobby of the hospital. Justin had called out to her, and she had sighed, dreading the daunting task of explaining her absence from work. The breakup with Damian flooded back to her, and the fact she was pregnant with Damian's baby hit her like a ton of bricks. "Pregnant?" was all Jane could say. "I was pregnant?"

"Yes. But it was in one of your fallopian tubes, and it ruptured. It caused you a lot of pain and severe bleeding. I was so scared I was going to lose you." Lauren paused as the feelings of not knowing if Jane was going to live or not resurfaced. Lauren's eyes filled with tears once again, and she took Jane's hand as the two friends sat in contemplative silence together. Jane quietly cried as her mind spun with thoughts about Damian, being pregnant with his baby, and now losing it. Everything was so emotionally overwhelming. She not only lost Damian, but she also lost his baby as well. How was she going to get over this? Over Damian? The hurricane of thoughts and worries quickly dissipated like smoke into thin air when a doctor entered the room. Embarrassed to be seen crying by a stranger, Jane wiped her tears away with the back of her hand.

He kindly greeted her. "Miss "Riley, how are you doing? My name is Dr. Thomas. I performed your emergency surgery today. I just wanted to stop by and see how you are doing and if you need anything. I understand you are a nurse here and probably have some questions for me."

Dr. Thomas explained everything to Jane as she lay in bed and listened intently to his every word. But the only part of what he said that echoed as loud as a bomb exploding in her mind was that she was pregnant! Pregnant with Damian's baby! Not only did she lose the man she loved and adored with all her heart, but his legacy was also gone as well. *Damian's baby. She was pregnant.* The words wouldn't stop repeating on a vicious loop.

"Miss Riley? I'm prescribing some medication to manage the pain and keep you comfortable, but we need to have you up walking for short periods. It is important to move. I will come to check on you in the morning and see how you are doing. It is ok to eat as long as you are not feeling nauseated, but just in case, I'll put in an order for Zofran. Try to get some rest tonight." He rose and proceeded towards the door. For a brief moment, the doctor paused and then sympathetically expressed, "I'm sorry for your loss, Miss Riley."

Dr. Thomas's words hit her like a blow to the abdomen, making it hard for her to breathe. How she wished her thoughts would silence themselves. She didn't feel up to talking anymore. Lauren wasn't ready to talk and, honestly, didn't feel like it. Both women didn't say a word, recognizing they both needed the quiet time. Neither knew what to say. Jane felt numb with everything that had happened and the resulting emotions, which ravaged her heart. After several minutes passed, Jane whispered, "Lauren?"

"What's up?" Lauren tentatively smiled.

"Thank you for being here with me." Jane smiled back at Lauren.

"I wouldn't be anywhere else. I love you."

"I love you too," Jane said.

"You must be hungry. Why don't I go get us something to eat?"

Jane nodded. She wasn't hungry, truth be told, but she desired a few precious minutes to herself. She felt weary from the events of the last several days. The surgery, and now knowing she was pregnant with Damian's baby, made her head spin as an intense pain ravaged her heart and soul. Instinctively, Jane's hand rested on her abdomen, where once their baby grew, the baby she lost. Tears tumbled down her cheeks uncontrollably as sobs heaved from her chest.

Jane didn't hear her cell notification ring from the locker across from the bed. Little did she know, Gabriel had messaged.

Jane, raincheck on coffee? I'll catch up with you another day. I hope you had a good day.

Chapter 7

With a couple of sandwiches and coffees in hand, Lauren walked down the hall towards the unit where she had left Jane sleeping. Her cell phone chimed with a new text message, but with her hands full, she looked for a place to sit and see who it was. Sitting in a quiet area, Lauren looked at her phone to see a message from Damian. "What an ass!" she whispered to herself. It was clear to her he didn't care about Jane or the fact that she lost his baby and nearly died. Lauren knew it would destroy Jane to hear his complete disregard for her well-being and would only add to the nightmares she knew Jane regularly had. As Lauren reread his message, she decided it was best to keep this to herself and not tell Jane she'd reached out to Damian. She glanced at the single sentence.

We broke up. Jane isn't my problem anymore.

The last thing Lauren wanted was for Jane to see a message from him; it would destroy her, especially now, having just lost his baby. Lauren needed to ensure he hadn't called or texted Jane, and she walked to the small closet to find Jane's cell phone and cautiously opened her purse. Lauren looked back at Jane, who continued to sleep undisturbed, completely unaware of Lauren's attempt to protect her from further heartbreak.

She found Jane's phone and looked at the call list. There were no recent calls to or from Damian. But there was one unread text message, which she immediately opened, in case it was from Damian. But to Lauren's surprise, it wasn't from him; it was one from Gabriel Lockhart. Confused as to why he would message her, Lauren scrolled through the many messages they exchanged, and Lauren realized they were friends. *That's odd.* Lauren wondered why Jane never mentioned this to her. They had shared almost everything since they were ten years old. "Oh no," Lauren caught herself saying out loud. They were supposed to meet for coffee earlier that day. Now what was she supposed to do with this information? Let Gabriel think Jane never saw it? But Jane could not communicate with anyone, and if they were friends, he would want to know why she didn't meet with him.

It was entirely out of character for her to be so unsure of what to do. Whether at work or in her daily life, Lauren was used to people coming to her for advice. But at this moment, she had no idea what to do and wished she could ask someone. Should she call Gabriel now or let Jane tell him once she was home and feeling better? As Lauren read his message a few more times, it became clear to her: the only right thing was to contact Gabriel. As she looked over at Jane's eerily peaceful body lying in bed, she knew it was the right decision deep down, and yes, Jane would have objected. But that didn't matter. Lauren stepped out of Jane's hospital room, walked to the nearby seating area, and called Gabriel.

"Hello, Jane," Gabriel said. "I'm sorry we couldn't meet up today, but I am happy you called."

"Ah, hi Gabriel, it's Lauren actually," she said hesitantly. "Sorry, I saw you messaged Jane, and I wanted to let you know what's happened and why Jane couldn't meet you."

"Oh, hi, Lauren. Ok. What do you mean let me know what's happened?" he questioned with concern.

Lauren breathed out a long, heavy sigh to gather the courage to tell him. "She was admitted into the hospital this afternoon. I didn't want you to think she stood you up. Things deteriorated between her and Damian, and they broke up a couple of weeks ago. I wasn't sure if they were talking to one another, and I reached out to him. But when I checked to see if he replied, I saw your message. I didn't realize you two were friends." Lauren waited for his response, curious what he would say.

Gabriel paused a moment and processed what he had just heard. Jane was in the hospital, but why? All he wanted to know from Lauren was what happened. Before Gabriel could say anything, though, he couldn't dismiss the quiet sobbing he heard on the other end of the line. What happened to Jane consumed his thoughts, but he had to be patient with Lauren, as she was obviously upset. Rather than interrogate her on the phone, Gabriel decided it would be best to talk when he got to the hospital. With that in mind, he said, "I'll come right down. Can I bring anything for you?" Gabriel asked.

Appreciative of his concern, Lauren replied quietly, "No, but thank you. You don't have to come down, really. I just thought you should know why Jane couldn't meet you."

"I want to see her. What room is she in?" Gabriel asked.

Lauren paused momentarily and pondered why he felt so adamant about seeing Jane. She determined it wasn't for her to decide for him. "She's in room 611."

"Thank you for letting me know, Lauren. I appreciate it. See you soon."

Lauren sat in silence for several minutes, contemplating if she did the right thing or not. But she couldn't help but wonder why he took such an interest in Jane. He and Brooke had been together for some time. Maybe things were rocky between them. Lauren shook her head in uncertainty as she stood up. Perhaps a walk would help clear her head and stop the overthinking, which hijacked her every thought. For the sake of her best friend, Lauren couldn't let on she didn't trust him. Jane, at that moment, needed all the support she could give.

A short time later, Gabriel walked into the hospital and immediately looked up. The glass walls seemed to be built mostly of glass, which allowed the starry night sky to take centre stage. Gabriel marvelled at the idea of Jane seeing this picturesque view every day she worked. It seemed odd to see so many people coming and going during this time in the evening. But he wished to be there under different circumstances, for Gabriel's mind was preoccupied with troublesome thoughts of Jane as he walked to the elevators.

Once on the sixth floor, he glanced around for Jane's room; however, it wasn't in sight. Gabriel walked down the hall to find someone to ask. Random beeping sounds from medical equipment echoed in the background, making him feel uneasy deep inside. The idea of Jane being connected to such machines made him sick to his stomach and filled his heart with worry. He just wished he could find where Jane was. Much to Gabriel's relief, a nurse sat at a desk writing in a chart as he approached. "Hello, could I trouble you for some help, please? I was wondering if you could tell me where I can find Jane Riley's room?

"Visiting hours are almost over at 9:00 p.m. Are you family?" one of the nurses asked with a hint of curiosity she wasn't at all ashamed of showing.

"I am a friend of Jane's," Gabriel said with a look of concern.

The nurse saw the concern shade the handsome stranger's face and said, "We know Jane. She is a lovely girl. She is just down the hall, first door on your right."

"Thank you," he replied and walked away from the desk down the hall.

Gabriel walked down the hall, passing by other visitors as his mind raced with thoughts of what to expect. He quietly approached the partially opened door of Jane's hospital room. With his hand on the door handle, Gabriel paused before entering as he realized Jane was not alone. Quietly, he stood off to the side and listened to the man, whom he recognized from the uniform to be a security guard from the hospital. Why would he be there with Jane, he wondered. He saw the man take one of Jane's fragile hands in his, hesitantly place a kiss upon it, and gently stroke her hair. Gabriel didn't know who this man was, but he had no intention of letting anything happen to Jane while she lay helpless in the hospital bed. It was time for him to leave, and he opened the door fully. "Oh, sorry, I thought Jane was alone," Gabriel said innocently.

Startled, the young man seemed flustered, like a small kid caught doing something they shouldn't be. "Oh, I was just leaving," the tall, dark-haired man in uniform said. "I'm Justin, a friend of Jane's. I came to see how she was doing."

But Gabriel couldn't shake the feeling of distrust about him. This so-called friend needed to leave; now, Gabriel thought to himself. "It was nice of you to check on her. When she wakes up, I'll let her know you were here," Gabriel stated in a low, controlled voice, knowing he had no intention of doing anything of the sort.

"Great. Thanks." Justin retreated quickly, unsure if the man saw anything before he entered the room.

"Good night," Gabriel said as Justin hurried past him on his way out of the room. Finally, alone, Gabriel lost all interest in the young man as he walked towards Jane's peaceful body lying in bed, thankful she was safe. Taking a seat beside her bed and never taking his eyes off her face, he saw how pale her skin was and couldn't ignore the wires connected to her chest or the oxygen tubing in her nose. Never before had he seen anyone look so fragile. Nothing could have prepared him to see how defenceless she appeared, and it made him sick to his stomach, knowing that creep Justin was near her.

How he wished she would open her eyes and say something to ease his worries that troubled his heart. Despite knowing she needed her rest, desperation stirred deep within him to see Jane open her eyes, even for a brief moment. From where he sat, he whispered, "Jane."

But she remained asleep and completely unaware of his presence. Voices in the hall distracted Gabriel, causing him to glance back at the door, half expecting someone to walk into the room. But the people soon passed, and he remained alone with Jane, desperately needing her to open her eyes. He stood up and leaned closer to her lifeless body and whispered in her ear, "Jane? You need to wake up. It's Gabriel." His eyes intently watched her face for some sign she knew he was there. "Jane, please, open your eyes for me," he pleaded while he tenderly caressed her cheek.

That voice called out to her in her head again, "Jane, wake up." But she couldn't. Oh, God, was she paralyzed? Or worse, was she dead? *Noooo!* she silently screamed. What happened to her? Why couldn't she move? Jane tried again with all her might to move, but it was hopeless. Her body wouldn't listen. She felt drained of any energy as the exhaustion pulled her deep into its grip, making it difficult to wake up and too much to fight. A moment later, the voice in her head went silent.

Gabriel sat back down by Jane's bedside, holding her hand. Even though he knew she was alive, as evidenced by the heart monitor connected to her and the warmth of her breath, he just didn't understand why she wasn't awake. For the first time Gabriel could ever recall in his life, he felt lost in what to do or how to help. The feeling of helplessness was overwhelming. As the minutes passed, Gabriel grew impatient and decided to try one more time to encourage Jane to open her eyes. As he stood beside her, he wished with all he had that Jane would show some sign she would be ok. But as he gazed at Jane, his heart filled with dread at the possibility she wouldn't wake up. A deep, heavy sigh filled his chest as he put his hands on Jane's shoulders. "Jane, wake up, please. Open your eyes. It's Gabriel. I'm here with you."

There was that voice again calling out to her. Damian, she thought to herself. The calm serenity beckoned to her, surrounded her, and where ever that was, she didn't care. It was so peaceful. But that voice kept calling to her, and it was hard to drown it out. Maybe it was Damian. It had to be him. He did care about her, after all. Damian was there! Suddenly, the idea of sleep was the furthest thing from Jane's mind; she needed to see him, to tell him how much she missed him. With every ounce of energy Jane could gather, she tried to open her eyes, but they were heavy and sealed closed. Why couldn't she wake up? She tried to open her mouth and call out to him, but all that came out was something more recognizable as a moan. Why was this so hard? What was wrong with her?

Gabriel felt a sudden jolt deep in his heart when Jane quietly groaned. She heard him. He couldn't give up now. He knew he was close to getting Jane to open her eyes; he could feel it. Gabriel slid one arm under Jane's shoulders as he sat down beside her on the bed. Cradling her in his arm, caressing her cheek, Gabriel whispered, "Jane, open your eyes. Come back to me."

The warmth of his body felt heavenly as the sound of his gentle voice called out to her, begging her to come back to him. "I'm trying," Jane pleaded slightly. "I'm trying." Jane's eyes flickered open for the briefest moment before they closed shut once again. But she told herself to keep going as she desperately wanted to see Damian's face, to feel his touch, run her hand through his thick hair, and smell his rousing cologne. Jane earnestly wanted to open her eyes.

"Jane, wake up." She heard the voice firmly command. At that moment, an incredible brightness flooded her sight, blinding Jane's eyes as they flickered open. It was almost unbearable and not something she could have prepared for, and she quickly shut them tight once again.

That's it, Jane, open your eyes again for me." Gabriel softly caressed her cheek.

"Damian." Jane tried calling out, but some unrecognizable sound left her lips, adding to her frustration. The warmth of his hand against her skin drew her towards him, like a moth to a flame. Jane was determined to move and see him. "Wake up!" she commanded herself. Her eyes fluttered open, where Jane saw a brief but blurred glimpse of a man hovering near her as she tried to focus and adjust to the brilliant light. Jane, however, shut her eyes tightly from the extreme brightness, but it didn't deter her from fighting against the innate instinct to close them tightly.

"Jane, you're awake!" Gabriel exclaimed with happiness as he hugged her gently, and relief flooded his heart. "It's Gabriel," he whispered in her ear.

"Hi." A very hoarse, weak voice left her lips. Her body was still unable to move as much as she ardently wanted. All Jane wanted was to reciprocate Damian's touch, and she tried to move her hand, but only her fingers seemed to work.

"Jane, I'm so happy you are awake. You're ok," Gabriel said, smiling while he looked into her eyes.

Ok? Why wouldn't I be, ok? Everything was so foggy, and she couldn't focus. Jane lay still as the confusion clouded her ability to reason and left her feeling scared. "What?" was all Jane whispered as she tried to focus her vision. "Damian?" she called out in a whisper.

A piercing pain stabbed Gabriel in the chest as Jane said Damian's name. "No, Jane, it's Gabriel." Despite his disappointment, Gabriel let it all go. Experiencing so much trauma in the recent past, Gabriel knew he wasn't fully aware of the details, and he needed to give Jane some grace. Gratitude, mixed with a sigh of relief, made him thankful he was with her when Jane opened her eyes. The thought of her being alone when she awoke made him feel uneasy, as he knew she would have been confused and scared. These feelings he never wanted Jane to experience around him.

Jane's vision cleared up enough for her to see that she was not in her bed, not at Lauren's condo, and Damian was not beside her. "Gabriel?" Jane questioned in a whisper. *Why would he be here?* She was not sure what to say to him. Jane realized it wasn't Damian, after all, who had called out to her. This reminded Jane, once again, that he didn't care about her. Tears misted over her eyes as disappointment welled up inside for wasting any hope on a man who didn't give a damn about her. Embarrassed by her emotional state, once again, in front of Gabriel, Jane turned her head away from him.

"Jane, please do not turn away from me; there is no need to hide your feelings from me. I can't imagine what you are going through, but I am here for you. You are ok; you are safe," he said quietly and reached out to wipe away a tear from her cheek with the back of his hand.

Jane couldn't form the words, and her mind swirled with questions as she looked about the unrecognizable, yet somewhat familiar, surroundings. She was so confused. Why was he here? Who called him, and why? Jane looked around and realized, finally, she was in a hospital room, but why? What happened to her? Her hand reached up and took off the oxygen from her nose as she surveyed the room and saw the cardiac monitor, a blood pressure cuff on her upper arm, and a bandage on her abdomen. A sense of panic hit her like a bolt of lightning.

"Jane," Gabriel said out loud as he took Jane by her shoulders in the hopes of interrupting her panic. "You are in the hospital. Something happened today, and you had to have surgery. He searched her face for any sign of remembrance of what caused her to be in the hospital after having emergency surgery, but confusion clouded Jane's pretty features. Do you remember anything, Jane?" He searched her face for any sign of recollection of the events earlier that day.

I remember getting ready for work, but that is...." and her voice trailed off as the softness of her beautiful face clouded over with confusion. "I had surgery?" Jane questioned, looking directly at Gabriel for an answer.

"Yes, Jane. I'm sorry, but I don't know what happened today to give you any answers. Lauren has been here all day with you, but I think she took a break for a bit. I have no doubt she will be able to tell you everything.

"What day is it?" Jane silently questioned. Then it dawned on her, she was supposed to meet Gabriel for coffee, but then everything changed, preventing her from being able to message him. "Crap," she whispered.

"What?" Gabriel asked.

Jane bashfully looked at Gabriel and said, "I think we were meeting for coffee. I'm sorry."

Gabriel smiled and said in a teasing tone, "No need to apologize. It wasn't like you were avoiding me." He gave a sly smile that made Jane's heart race, evident to them both on the monitor.

There was no hiding the effect Gabriel had upon her, it seemed. Jane felt her cheeks flush, and she cast her eyes down from the sudden embarrassment she couldn't hide. Clearing her throat and fidgeting with the blanket, unsure of what to say, Jane decided there was no point avoiding the obvious any longer. "Can I ask how you found out I was here?"

Gabriel leaned against the windowsill, looking into Jane's curious, blue eyes, "Lauren messaged me. She saw the text I sent to you about our coffee date and wanted me to know where you were," he teased.

Did she just hear him right? Did he just call their meet-up a date? Was it? Or perhaps, it was only a slip of words. Jane fiddled with the sensor on her finger while she tried to understand why Gabriel was with her now. As much as she appreciated him being there, a part of her wondered, why?

Gabriel saw how Jane was wrestling with something in her mind, but he also knew she wouldn't feel comfortable asking what was coursing through her mind if he pushed her. Instead, he wanted her to know she was safe being with him and could tell him anything. "Jane, you can ask me anything. What's on your mind?"

She smiled but kept her eyes cast down as she fiddled with the sensor. Lost in thought, the sudden, shrill alarm going off from removing the sensor from her finger jolted Jane back to the real world. Embarrassed, she quickly put it back on her finger. "Why are you here? I'm, um, not sure why, that's all." She felt uncertain of herself and wasn't sure if she was ready to hear his answer. Jane knew what she wished to hear; however, that was impossible.

"I couldn't imagine not being here for you or Lauren. She sounded troubled on the phone, and after we chatted a few minutes, she filled me in that you were in surgery. I appreciated her letting me know. I hope that was ok?" he sincerely asked.

As Jane thought about what it must have been like for Lauren, she felt a sense of guilt run through her. She hadn't considered what it was like for her, knowing she had been a burden upon Lauren the past couple of months. And now this.

"Lauren wasn't here when you came?" Jane questioned.

"No, she probably went for a walk," Gabriel said. "She hasn't left your bedside since you got out of recovery."

"Oh," was all Jane could say as the guilt ravished her heart.

"I don't think anything would have kept her away, Jane. She was right where she needed to be, with you."

"Where was who?" Lauren excitedly asked as she entered the room. One look at Jane awake was the best thing Lauren had seen all day. Unable to control herself, she rushed over and hugged her best friend. "You have no idea how happy I am to see you awake. You scared me to death."

"I'm so sorry, Lauren. I didn't mean to worry you," Jane said as tears tumbled down her cheeks. "I'm really sorry."

"Oh, Jane, you don't need to apologize. You did nothing wrong. I can be scared for you if I want," she sassily said and wiped the stray tears along Jane's cheek with her finger. "Stop with the tears, you're going to make me cry, and I simply can't have that in the presence of a man," Lauren teased.

Jane blushed and realized, yes, Gabriel was still in the room. God, she was such a baby lately.

"Thank you for coming here, Gabriel," Lauren said.

"My pleasure. Can I get either of you anything?"

Both women shook their heads no. With that, Gabriel got up from the windowsill and took Jane's hand in his. "I'll let you two catch up. I'll come by tomorrow for a visit."

"Ok," said Jane while distracted by the site of her hand in his. Its warmth, its strength, made her heart race once again. *Damn machines*, she thought to herself as she couldn't hide her feelings from the monitor.

"Thank you again for coming this evening, Gabriel," Lauren said.

Gabriel walked toward the door, pausing briefly before opening it. "I want you to get some sleep tonight, Jane." His handsome face showed concern while his voice had an edge of dominance, almost like an order. As if Lauren read Jane's thoughts, she teasingly asked with a smirk, "Is that an order, Doctor?"

Gabriel smiled without saying a word or shifting his gaze away from Jane's eyes. He knew the effect he had upon her and the one she had upon him, which was strangely becoming more apparent. His intrigue for Jane was ever-growing with each encounter they shared, with every glance, or downcast eyes and shy smile sent his way. Her submissive heart aimed to please him. His inclination to protect Jane was something he felt grow with each interaction, feeding his dominant ego. This feeling Gabriel wasn't able to push aside or ignore, like he used to, since meeting Jane.

Jane's heart pounded in her chest as Gabriel's piercing dark eyes bore deep into her soul. She found him both intimidating and intriguing. The very touch of his hand made her feel like there was no one else around, just Gabriel and her. He clouded her ability to think straight and made her feel like she mattered and was safe. But why? He was with Brooke. So why was he here with her this night?

"Good night, Jane. Please get some sleep tonight," Gabriel requested with an unyielding gaze.

Disappointing Gabriel was the last thing she wanted to do, but what compelled her to want to gratify? Afraid to speak and give away her desire to please him, Jane decided to nod instead.

With a smile, Gabriel said, "I'll see you tomorrow. Thank you again for calling me, Lauren."

Jane had no idea how he felt when she let her submissive persona shine. She naturally embodied a docile ego with an inner courage, an ever-endearing heart, and a gentle soul. She had intelligence, resiliency, and beauty. All these characteristics made Jane remarkably charming to him in every way. Since the night of the engagement party, after they had talked in the garden, his lavish interest to learn more about her had only grown each time they connected. He saw within her an alluring vulnerability he hadn't seen in a woman in some time. Being around like-minded people every day, and even in his relationship with Brooke, Gabriel kept his intimate, dominant side hidden deep within. Brooke was an independent businesswoman, whom he admired greatly, but knew she was far from being submissive. She wasn't capable of being vulnerable in the ways a Dom values most, and in many cases needs, to create a synergy with opposite spirits. Brook's independence was far from being a fault. Rather, it was the reason she was so successful, amongst many other traits she possessed. Brooke was a lovely partner to have, and he was always appreciative of her being in his life.

While Gabriel drove back to the brewery, he pondered the idea of exercising the Dom in himself in an intimate way, rather than just being the boss, operating his business and managing the staff. It had been several years since he had allowed himself to explore these deep-seated feelings, as the distractions of real-life took a firm hold on his daily routine. Then, as if getting a push from fate itself, a submissive woman named Jane Riley walked into his life, a uniquely rare gift for a Dom such as himself.

Chapter 8

Lauren woke up feeling exhausted and somewhat overwhelmed by all the events of the last few days and going back and forth from the hospital. Her usual get up and go just wasn't there as her desire to get out of bed lost out to the seduction of the soft warmth she felt around her. If it weren't for the decadent aroma of a perfectly brewed pot of coffee beckoning Lauren to get up, she would have hibernated all day in the comfort of her 1000 thread count Egyptian cotton sheets, relishing the quiet moments to herself. However, this morning, someone else had different plans in mind. Lauren's cell phone chimed with a new text message. Thinking it was either her fiancé Steve or Jane, she was surprised to see it was neither of them. Instead, it was Brooke. It read,

Hey, can we could talk?

Lauren paused briefly, then messaged,

Of course.

Almost as soon as she sent the message, Lauren's phone rang while still in her hand. "Hi, are you ok?"

"I'm ok. I just wanted to talk to you about something. I feel embarrassed, even bringing it up," said Brooke.

Lauren tried to remember a situation in which she found Brooke feeling embarrassed, and she couldn't recall a single time.

It was an odd thing for her to say, let alone admit. Something was going on for sure. "Brooke, what's wrong?" Lauren questioned.

"Have you ever been jealous of anyone?" Brooke asked hesitantly. She breathed out a deep sigh as though she had been holding her breath. She couldn't believe she was even saying those words out to her best friend.

Lauren couldn't help but think to herself why Brooke was feeling jealous, piquing her interest. But rather than answering Brooke's question, Lauren instead chose to ask her own, "What's happened?"

"Nothing. I'm just being stupid." However, Brooke wasn't even convinced by her own words, as jealousy burrowed deep within and conspired with her mind to further pursue the conversation. "Have you ever known someone who was attracted to two people at the same time?"

"Ahhh, no, can't say I have. Are you interested in someone else?"

Brooke lowered her head, unable to utter the words to herself, let alone to her best friend. She simply couldn't let herself say them.

Brooke's silence was deafening to Lauren, making her answer glaringly apparent. "Who would Gabriel be interested in with you in his life?" No sooner had the words left her lips when Lauren paused for a brief moment as her consciousness answered her question. Jane.

Brooke envisioned the look of realization crossing Lauren's face before saying, "You see it between them too." A heavy sigh didn't relieve the pressure Brooke felt in her chest as she finally said it for herself, "Gabriel wants Jane."

The truth was, Lauren did see Gabriel's interest in Jane. She wasn't sure exactly when things began to change for him, but Lauren knew Jane to be soft-hearted and even gullible at times. In Lauren's opinion, these traits often left her vulnerable, and with some kind, attentive gestures from a handsome man like Gabriel, Lauren had no doubts that Jane felt special and flattered.

Given how exposed her friend's heart was about everything with Damian and her recent, devastating loss of his baby, she could see how tempting Gabriel could be. But Lauren couldn't dismiss the obligation she felt to tell Brooke about Jane, even if she didn't want to hear it. "I'm not sure if you have heard or not about Jane," Lauren said hesitantly.

"What about her? If you mean about her and Damian breaking up? Yes, I've heard. It doesn't give her the right to my boyfriend just because she can't keep her own," Brooke stated with furry.

Lauren paused, unsure of how to explain things to Brooke. The last thing she wanted to do was hurt her and provoke Brooke further into hating Jane and distrusting Gabriel.

"Lauren, just tell me." Brooke blurted out.

"Gabriel was at the hospital tonight. He was there to see Jane."

"What? What do you mean he was at the hospital? Why wouldn't he tell me he was hurt?" Brooke yelled out loudly. "What happened, Lauren?" she demanded.

"Brooke, no. Gabriel is fine; it's about Jane." Lauren said hesitantly.

"What about her? Did she have another fight with Damian? So, what else is new?" Brooke lashed out.

"Brooke, Jane had emergency surgery for an ectopic pregnancy. I left to get a coffee, and when I came back to her room, Gabriel was there."

Brooke felt like she was punched in the stomach as she tried to catch her breath. Anger fueled by jealousy boiled deep at the very thought Gabriel was by Jane's side. "What do you mean he was there? How would he have known Jane was in the hospital?"

Lauren recalled only a handful of times she saw Brooke emotional, but this situation was very different from any previous outburst. She was angry and jealous, something Lauren never expected from Brooke. How was she supposed to tell Brooke? As she took a deep breath in, Lauren knew what she was about to say would hurt her friend, but she had the right to know. "Brooke,

I told him. He and Jane were supposed to meet for coffee that afternoon, but she collapsed in the hospital lobby on her way to work, and she went into emergency surgery. I sent a text to Damian telling him, and a while later, I saw a text message on Jane's cell and thought it was from Damian. I thought he deserved to know Jane was in surgery and had lost their baby. But it wasn't him. It was Gabriel."

Brooke's anger saturated her heart and every word from her lips as Lauren's betrayal sank in. How dare you encourage Gabriel to meet with Jane. Why was Lauren treating Jane like she was so innocent and hadn't done anything wrong? Why was Jane's failed relationship with Damian more relevant, or rather the only excuse Jane could come up with to see Gabriel, despite being very aware of her relationship with him? Brooke's ability to contain her fury had become near impossible. "Why the hell would you reply to Gabriel's text and tell him about the woman he is cheating on me with?"

Lauren knew Brooke was angry, and rightfully so, but she didn't count on being in the middle of Brooke's insecurities and Jane's unfortunate life situations. She honestly thought she had done the right thing, given the circumstances, but it seemed Lauren was wrong despite her honest intentions. Guess there was only one thing to do.

"Brooke, I'm sorry. It wasn't my intention to hurt you. I thought I was doing the right thing, and I didn't realize how it would make you feel. For some reason, they are friends. I can't believe Jane would do anything to jeopardize or be any threat to your relationship with Gabriel. How could he not love you, Brooke? You are successful and gorgeous. What more could he possibly want? Brooke remained silent on the other end of the line, but Lauren knew she was listening to her every word. "Brooke, please don't be mad at me. I didn't tell him to upset you. Please know that."

Brooke did know it deep down; she just didn't want to admit it. Gabriel was a kind man, and she knew he had talked to Jane before. Jane's life was a complete disaster, and for whatever reason, Gabriel had an interest in her. She also had a secret that Brooke hadn't told anyone yet, including Gabriel or Lauren.

"Brooke, please talk to me?" Lauren begged.

She was going to have to find the courage to tell Lauren and Gabriel sooner than later. Brooke drew in a deep breath and decided it was now or never before she changed her mind and lost her nerve. "Lauren, I have to tell you something."

Lauren hesitated, unsure of what to say, as she wondered what Brooke was going to tell her. Today had been a day of unforeseen surprises, and Lauren wasn't sure if she was up for anymore. She knew deep down, though, she didn't have a choice. "Ok..." Lauren said with hesitation.

"I'm moving to England. I got the promotion to head the European division, and I decided to take it. I haven't told anyone yet, except you."

"That is amazing news. I didn't even know you applied, but you've worked so hard, and I'm not surprised at all you got it. I'm so happy for you!"

"Thanks, but I am still mad at you," Brooke blurted over the phone, slightly pouting.

"Brooke, I didn't mean to hurt you. You have to believe me."

Brooke did believe her, but it still didn't change how she felt about Jane and the resulting frustrations. "Argh! Jane, the perpetually helpless child in distress. You would think she could find a man of her own to fix her problems. Of course, Gabriel is going to be attracted to her helplessness, a routine she has down pat. Men like him find the damsel in distress routine appealing, I suppose, and want to fix everything wrong in their life. But he is my boyfriend! It pisses me off that Jane would have him wrapped around her finger. And now, I'm taking a promotion and moving to London. How am I going to leave knowing he and Jane could start seeing one another? Maybe I should break up with him. That way, he can fuck her all he wants without me being in the picture!" Brooke rambled in anger but felt vindicated she was heard.

Disappointed in Brooke's lack of empathy for Jane, Lauren knew there was no point in trying to change her mind, given how she felt and her state of mind. It will be hard for Brooke to leave Gabriel and San Fransisco, where her entire life was, to go to a new country and job. When she weighed the benefits of saying what was really on her mind, Lauren knew it wasn't worth it, even at the expense of her dear friend, Jane. It was best to let it go for everyone's sake.

"Brooke, you have worked so hard for this amazing promotion, and you should be proud of yourself. All the work you have put into the company doesn't compare with what you've accomplished taking care of yourself. You are not the same woman that you were when you first moved to San Fransisco. I remember when you first walked into the office and had met everyone. Not sure if I ever told you this before, but I was so envious of you. You were already a star in the advertising world, and I saw you as competition. Then I got to know you and saw all of the great work you did, and I realized your drive to succeed was something to learn from rather than be jealous of. You earned this promotion, and the London team won't know what hit them. That is guaranteed, but is your relationship with Gabriel? Is he going to wait for you? Is he your "one"? You have fifteen years within the firm and about six months with Gabriel. I can't even pretend to understand what is going through your mind and heart, but you need to tell Gabriel soon."

Brooke heard her friend's words and knew exactly what needed to happen; Lauren was right. She needed to talk to Gabriel.

"I know." a heavy sigh left Brooke's chest.

"Brooke, you do know you deserve this promotion, right?"

"I don't know, Lauren." Brooke sighed. "Is it possible I got it because I am a woman, or did I earn it? I know there will be numerous rumours around the office about how I "earned" the promotion by sleeping my way through the upper executive. And then there is Gabriel; will we be able to do the long-distance relationship thing? Will he accept me moving away?

"Brooke, you can't predict what he is going to say or do. You have to talk to him," Lauren said

"I know, I know." Brooke no longer felt like talking and said, "I'll call you later, ok?"

The two friends said their goodbyes, and Brooke lay down, staring at the ceiling. She couldn't delay it any longer, she decided and picked up her cell phone. "Hi, are you going to be home after work tonight? Maybe we could make dinner and watch a movie or something tonight. Sounds great. I'll see you tonight."

Staring blankly up at the ceiling, Brooke couldn't escape the uncertainty about her future both with the move professionally and her relationship with Gabriel.

"Dinner was great, thank you," Brooke said, taking the last sip of her wine.

"Would you like more wine?" Gabriel asked, pausing before pouring more into Brooke's glass.

"Mmm, yes, please."

Gabriel sat beside Brooke, wrapping one arm around her shoulders, breathing in the heady scent of her perfume. The temptation of Brooke's feminine allure was too great for even the likes of Gabriel to resist as his fingertips trailed down from her shoulder to her hand before interlacing his fingers with hers. Brooke felt the warmth of his breath against the sensitive skin of her neck as he slowly kissed along it. Craving to feel and taste his kisses, Brooke turned her head, but just before their lips met, she felt his hand fist her hair, pulling slightly backward, preventing her from being able to move her head.

"Hey, what's that for?" she whined.

"I'm not done yet," Gabriel huskily whispered into Brooke's ear.

"But I want to kiss you," Brook cooed.

"Not yet, patience, my love."

Brooke grew discouraged at the notion she couldn't kiss him but played along, hoping it wouldn't be long before she could taste him. She soon got her wish, and they embraced, kissing and touching with fervour. Pushing away from Gabriel slightly, Brooke intently looked into his dark eyes, smiled a come-hither smile, and requested, "fuck me now."

Although Gabriel didn't particularly enjoy having demands made of him, he decided to give them both what they were craving. Brooke was used to being in charge and in control at all times, both in her business and personal life. But Gabriel craved to have her let her guard down when they were intimate in the hopes of discovering the kind of pleasure and freedom he wished Brooke to experience with him. Not having to decide what to do or where, only experiencing the desire and rapture he wanted to lavish upon her body. Freeing her mind of the cumbersome thoughts from her day, only to focus upon the euphoria of the multiple orgasms he hungered to elicit from her. He needed her, he wanted her, and he was going to fuck her.

Gabriel picked up Brooke with ease, carrying her towards the bed as she wrapped her legs around his waist and madly kissed him. Resting her upon the bed, Gabriel took her hands in his and slowly slid them above her head. The scent of Brooke's perfume cast its spell upon him, enticing him to want her even more. Without missing a beat, Gabriel moved both of Brooke's wrists into the grip of one hand, still enjoying their insatiable kisses as his other hand gradually began to undo the front of her blouse, one button at a time.

"I need you," Brooke whispered against Gabriel's lips.

"I know. I need you too, but first, I'm going to make you cum over and over and over again."

Brooke relished the idea of Gabriel making her cum so expertly in whatever way he desired. Gabriel was a gifted man in many ways and made her feel like a woman besieged by a thousand fireworks going off inside her body, leaving her quivering and breathless from each stupefying orgasm. The very thought of being so overcome with ecstasy made Brooke's head spin in anticipation and her pussy salaciously wet. Desperate to move her arms from above her head, Brooke tried to pull them free of Gabriel's grip; however, her trivial effort only left her frustrated as his hand tightened, holding her wrists firmly in place.

"I want to touch you," Brooke whined, trying to free herself once again.

"I'm not done with you yet," Gabriel huskily whispered.

No sooner did the words leave his lips when Brooke felt the front of her blouse opening, exposing a red, see-through bralette revealing her hard, erect nipples through the flimsy fabric. Gabriel's eroticism intensified as his tongue swirled over the see-through material, barely covering her voluptuous breasts. As Gabriel twirled round and round her nipples and hungrily sucked at the oversensitive flesh, Brooke's moans grew louder. She couldn't help but move her body beneath the weight of his, grinding her clit against his knee rhythmically, edging herself closer to rapture.

Gabriel's own feral hunger to make Brooke cum and feel her velvet wetness around his hard cock grew insatiable. Releasing her wrists, he lifted her lacy bra, freeing her breasts from the flimsy bondage. He lifted Brooke's short skirt over her hips, exposing a matching red thong and thigh-high stay-up stockings. The sight of her lying there, legs spread apart with her glistening sweet juices beckoning Gabriel to taste her was too much for him to resist, so he didn't. Kneeling at the edge of the bed, Gabriel spread Brooke's legs wider and pushed her knees up towards her chest, displaying her feminine essence to him.

"Ooooh, please," Brooke begged, her eyes closed, and soft murmurs escaped her lips. She slid her hands over the contours of her breasts, kneading them slowly, pinching her nipples. "Please."

"What do you desire me to do, my love?" Gabriel said, enthralled with watching Brooke touch herself, hearing her moans, and seeing her glistening wetness coat her inner thighs, casting a spell upon him to devour her with his tongue. But as a Dom, he'd learned the value of patience and taking his time. The power to control not only himself but the body and mind of a submissive was heady and exciting, especially with a very needy sub. Summoning suspense and lust-filled longing with an intimate partner was one of his favourite things, which fed his Dom ego's carnal urges to control. He was rock hard, and despite the bondage of his growing passionate needs, making his pants uncomfortable, it was time to make Brooke cum to life. "Brooke, tell me what you want me to do," he asked. Slowly, with one finger, he slid her thong to the side, revealing her desire. Along her inner thighs, Gabriel planted soft kisses and gentle bites to her sensitive skin, making Brooke moan loudly and squirm with great protest. He soon reached the most sumptuous softness, that of her pussy. His taunting kisses turned to sensual strokes of his tongue along her velvety wetness, making Brooke moan loudly.

"Oh, God, yes!" Brooke swooned. "Make me cum!"

Gabriel didn't approve of her demanding tone, so he stopped licking her juices. Instead, he reverted to kissing her thighs once again, asking in between kisses, "What do you say, Brooke?"

Frustrated with Gabriel stopping his lavish licking upon her throbbing pussy Brooke cried out, "Just make me cum!"

"Aren't you forgetting something? What do you say?" He scolded with a smirk on his face, knowing full well, Brooke was impatient and had such a pent-up need begging to be released by several orgasms.

Her frustrations couldn't be contained. "I need you to make me cum. Enough with the games! If you aren't going to make me cum while you are down there, then I'll get out my vibe and take care of business myself!"

Gabriel heard the anger in her voice and realized she wasn't about to succumb to his will. Despite the lack of submissiveness in her, he couldn't deny her need to release the tension he had created in her body. Brooke was not submissive and never would be, and that was ok. He still had every intention of enjoying himself, knowing he could make her body do what he willed it. With that in mind, the heavenly scent of her wetness beckoned to him. Long generous licks of his tongue found the small nub of her clit with ease, and he inserted one finger inside her, massaging her G-spot. Long broad licks paired with the rapidly rising need within her body, and Brooke trembled with every luxurious stroke of his tongue. Gabriel increased the speed of his licks upon her clit, skillfully knowing she was teetering closer to Nirvana, but he wasn't ready for that yet. As he circled his tongue around her clit, savouring her delectable sweetness, Gabriel began thrusting his finger, then two, deep inside Brooke, and she moved her hips in time with him. It was time. Robustly sucking on her clit and finger fucking her, Brooke's essence coated his fingers while her moans echoed loudly off the walls; she was so close.

"Don't stop!" She breathlessly gasped while teetering on the edge of a most sinfully arousing orgasm. "I'm cumming! I'm cumming!" Within seconds, Brooke's body trembled with the intense orgasm.

Gabriel stood up and licked Brooke's juices off his fingers before freeing himself from his denim confines. He scooped Brooke under her knees, lifting her towards him as she was still recovering from her orgasmic haze, and with one thrust, buried his shaft deep inside Brooke's silken pussy, feeling its embracing warmth around his cock. His own urge to cum was too distracting for Gabriel, and he began rhythmically fucking her.

Brooke was pulled out of her euphoric high, fully aware of the wondrous feeling of being filled. "Fuck me!" she yelled out loud.

Needing no further invitation, Gabriel fucked Brooke fiercely with an animalistic hunger he had seldomly experienced previously with her. His own orgasmic release was rapidly rising within him as his scrotum felt engorged, his cock felt rock hard, and electric-like impulses coursed through his body. With one final thrust, the rush of cum filled Brooke's pussy as Gabriel's growl filled the air, and his body went rigid. Holding himself firmly against Brooke, still buried to the hilt within her, he looked down upon her body in awe, seeing his seed trickle down her buttocks and onto the bed. He hadn't cum that hard in some time. He'd forgotten the rush that made him feel lightheaded and weak in the knees. The captivating sight of Brooke's gorgeous, post-orgasmic glow was something to behold, and he slowly pulled out, then lay beside her as they both enjoyed the quiet time in one another's arms.

As Gabriel lay peacefully, feeling relaxed as he caressed Brooke's hair, his thoughts wandered to how uncertain he was of Brooke's ability to pause her control when they made love or enjoyed a spontaneous, gotta-have-you kind of fuck. This night proved his doubts were not to be questioned; she would never be submissive enough to feed his Dom persona. He could never relinquish his control; it was an integral part of him that had gone a very long time without being exercised. He needed domination; he needed a submissive lover. Without any hesitation, he knew what, or perhaps more so, who he yearned for. Jane.

After several minutes lying in silence next to Gabriel, Brooke rolled over to see him gazing at her contentedly. She knew telling him about her promotion had to be done, but apprehension plagued her thoughts. Was this the right moment? Brooke decided it didn't really matter in the end. No time would ever be the right one to deliver the difficult news she was both ecstatic and insecure about. Letting out a long sigh, she looked into Gabriel's dark, raven eyes, and she whispered, "I have something I need to tell you." She paused for a moment, drew in a deep breath, and said, "I got promoted at work, but it means I have to move to England, and I've decided to take it."

Upon hearing her news, Gabriel studied Brooke, but she avoided making any kind of eye contact with him. The feeling in his heart was mixed. It was both a feeling of solitude and one of pride. It was an odd combination, he thought to himself and wondered why he wasn't more disappointed, or upset, or even sad. Deep down, Gabriel wholeheartedly believed that Brooke deserved it, for she was intelligent, demanded excellence of herself and others, and she wanted the opportunity. In his mind, there was no other option for Brooke, she had to take the promotion, and he would support her. Remaining silent, he leaned over and kissed her softly, then said, "I am very proud of you. Congratulations."

Brooke knew Gabriel was sincere, and even though they had shared a great evening, it would be their last. Turning to face him, Brooke stated, "I think we should talk."

Chapter 9

There were only a few things Gabriel found subdued the restlessness in his soul: lying quietly against the feminine warmth of a lover's body and feeling the freedom of being on a bike with the wind rushing by and the sun on his back. Normally, a morning's motorcycle ride with the engine's hum and the pavement's vibration provided a distraction, enabling a peace and quiet for the noise within. But on this day, despite the natural serenity of the fresh morning air and the ride, nothing seemed to pause or clear away his persistent thoughts of the past several days. One such thought was his inevitable breakup with Brooke. His thoughts about their relationship left him knowing that Brooke taking the once-in-a-lifetime opportunity was the best decision for her. He acknowledged her need to claim her place in the marketing world and, if he were honest with himself, their relationship left him feeling unfulfilled. It was as though they were both just present instead of capturing one another's heart in the way a man liked to feel desired. If he were to be completely honest with himself, they both understood they were not a forever couple, but rather a couple for right now. There were tears shed the evening they talked, and Gabriel felt the sadness of their end. There were no second thoughts with his decision to support Brooke and the amazing and well-deserved promotion she decided to take. They both agreed if she turned down the job, Brooke would eventually resent him and wonder how her life would have been if she had made a different decision. Despite their mutual heartbreak, they parted as friends with a warm hug and a promise to keep in touch.

As the sun's radiance shone brilliantly over the waking city, Gabriel's thoughts were not just of Brooke. They shifted to another woman he did feel connected to, Jane. Her vulnerability and kind heart made Jane appear weak to many around her, but Gabriel knew better. She and everyone else around her didn't realize that Jane's greatest strength was her vulnerability. Underestimating her self-worth hindered Jane's personal growth and prevented her from discovering her true self: a woman worthy and loved, not just by the people who knew her, but more importantly, herself. It was his hope with some time and guidance, Jane's view of herself would shift so that she would see her strengths and value and believe in them. After a few coffee meet-ups over the last several months, they had gotten to know one another, and he enjoyed their conversations. Her ability to genuinely, or perhaps, blindly care for others was something he struggled to understand. Maybe it was that he hadn't found someone he cared for enough in that way, someone he could love with complete trust, honesty, and acceptance. The trust Jane had already earned with him was surprising. Recognizing this, his curiosity for Jane grew. Jane possessed so many endearing qualities, but she had one which Gabriel believed, no one, including Jane, recognized within herself: her innate submissive side. This side of Jane enticed the Dom within him to the point he felt it nearly impossible not to muse about it.

The very pleasant wonderings of Jane being submissive interrupted the peacefulness of his morning ride most deliciously. While his imagination toyed with the possibility Jane was submissive and didn't know it, he nourished his dominant ego with pure unadulterated sexual excitement, leaving him hard and pleasantly uncomfortable during his ride. Gabriel's pulse raced as images of Jane kneeling before him ravaged his imagination. "Argh!" He shook his head and immediately thought about getting himself together before he crashed. Being in control was something Gabriel always prided himself on, that was until he began to see Jane for the alluring woman she really was.

Once at the office, Gabriel stared out across the bay, absently watching the commuters slowly making their way over the Golden Gate Bridge to begin their routine day. He was unable to escape the continuous reel of intoxicating thoughts about Jane and how the Dom within him would relish the privilege of training, growing, and loving a submissive so precious. There was one thought, though, that silenced his yearning: Jane had no idea what she indeed was. Would Jane be willing to truly hear him if they were to talk about her exploring her submissive side? Would she be willing to give herself enough grace to consider the possibilities of a life she deserved, one where she was cherished, valued, and protected? Or would she retreat into the faded radiance of a life once hoped for with Damian, blindly unaware of the precious gift she is?

As the first decadent sip of coffee touched his tongue, Gabriel imagined holding both the heart and mind of a treasured submissive in the palm of his hand, feeling her need to be his. As a Dom, being able to shape and grow a sub's inner confidence and self-worth, so she embraced her strengths and beauty both inside and out, thrived deep within him. He knew others would think of him as odd and perhaps even an abuser, but Gabriel was far from being any of these. Guiding Jane in all the wonders of submission wasn't something he would take for granted. Trust was earned and established through a continuously open and frank conversation about all of the essential elements of any D/s relationship. Their mutually respected boundaries, desires, and intimacy are what create a unique and rare bond between a Dom and his sub, the connection few in any relationship experience. As Gabriel thought more about Jane's internal conflict, it became clear why it clouded her perception of what a healthy and realistic bond was. Her idea of love came from a belief you fall in love, get married, have 3.2 kids, and of course, a family dog and a single-family home, all wrapped up in a white picket fence. The false idea of a generic vanilla storybook ending of "happily ever after" believing in for better, for worse, for richer, for poorer, in sickness and in health, to love and cherish till death do you part created such unrealistic expectations around love and connection. A lack of passion, paired with a lack of open communication, was most often the kryptonite of any relationship. The idea of being in a passionless vanilla connection, even with someone as great as Brooke, lacked the intensity he craved to feel. He realized Brooke was not "the one," yet they had been blindly going through the motions of a relationship, aware of the distance which had already grown between them, but neither one was willing to voice it out of fear or obligation. Both Jane and Brooke found themselves in a lacklustre and even troubled relationship, forcing them to look at what they truly wanted. Two strong and very different women, stuck within the confined beliefs of a storybook ending of what love was or had to be, unaware of the uniqueness a D/s communicative relationship could offer.

Until recently, Gabriel had not allowed himself to think about having another submissive to call his own, who he could protect, cherish, and love. That was until he met Jane. Ever since they talked the night of Lauren's engagement party in the garden, she unintentionally engaged his thoughts during the day and haunted his dreams at night. She awakened within the deepest depths of his soul, something few subs ever had, and now, he couldn't ignore the hunger for her any longer. The Dom in him needed to breathe again, feel, and yes, love.

A day of routine business meetings, endless phone calls, and managing his staff couldn't divert Gabriel's concern of how Jane was doing. It had been over a week since he saw her in the hospital. He thought it was best to give her some time to herself, given what trauma she had endured. They kept in touch by text messages, but it wasn't the same as seeing her eyes and hearing her voice. Would all that she lost inhibit Jane from opening her heart again to another man? Was it too soon? He was concerned about Jane and needed to see her. It was time to see her face to face if she felt strong enough to see him. Perhaps it would be too much pressure for her, so Gabriel decided to message Lauren instead.

Hi, it's Gabriel. Checking in to see how Jane is.

Moments later, Lauren replied.

She is sad.

Gabriel typed a reply and then paused before pressing send. He very much wanted to see Jane, but it wasn't about him; it was for her and what she needed.

Do either of you need anything? I can come by for a visit if she is up to one.

Lauren replied.

I'll see what she says and get back to you if that is ok?

Sounds good. Please say hi for me.

Several minutes later, his text notification chimed, and to Gabriel's surprise, it was from Jane.

Thank you for saying hi. Lauren said you were thinking of coming over to visit. I would enjoy that. I'm not doing much these days, LOL.

His heart was delighted and hopeful, and instantly he replied.

Great. How about tomorrow afternoon? Unless that is too soon.

No, it's fine. See you tomorrow.

I hope the flowers are not too cliché, Gabriel thought to himself as he patiently waited for the door to open. The deadbolt unlocked, and the door opened as his heart raced with anticipation of seeing Jane. A moment later, her incredible blue eyes were the first thing he saw welcoming him and a slight smile upon her pretty lips. His heart warmed at the mere sight of her.

"Hi. Come in," she said, and as their eyes met, Gabriel saw a flash of joy before she cast her eyes downwards. An awkward silence followed as Jane looked sheepishly down at her clothing and realized how she must look. Black sweat pants rolled up to mid-calf and a white T-shirt, hair pulled back into a ponytail, and no makeup. He took the time to see her; the least she could have done was look more presentable as she hid behind him and closed the door.

Gabriel saw how uncomfortable Jane was as she fidgeted with her shirt's hem and smoothed back her hair. He was captivated by her beauty, even if Jane couldn't see it. Compared to how he saw her last week, frail and sick, Jane was smiling, and it pleased him.

"Please come in. Thanks for coming to see me."

"I was wondering how you were doing, but I wasn't sure if you would be up for visitors yet. So, I'm pleased you are doing well." As the two sat down, Gabriel noticed Jane was still not up to her usual strength, with her pale skin and dark circles under her eyes, evidence of the healing and rest her body needed.

"Would you like something to drink?" Jane asked as she stood up. Jane immediately felt lightheaded and thinking she might faint made her unsteady on her feet. "Phew, I'm sorry," Jane said as she flopped back on the sofa and closed her eyes, hoping the feeling would dissipate.

Gabriel kneeled in front of Jane, taking one of her hands in his. "You don't have to apologize. What do you like in your coffee?" he asked, searching her face for any hint she felt a bit better.

Jane's pale skin flushed with embarrassment, but despite it, she saw concern cloud over his handsome face. *Jane! Really?!* ran through her mind. Feeling like a burden to Gabriel and everyone around who showed her kindness and patience, Jane couldn't ignore the gentle, comforting feeling of his hand around hers. He had no idea how safe he made her feel or how much she secretly adored and appreciated him being with her at that moment. But really, who was she kidding? How could a man like Gabriel Lockhart ever be interested in a woman like her? And more so, why would he be? As the all-too-familiar tug-of-war between her heart and head waged war upon her, Jane slowly withdrew her hand from Gabriel's, replying back, "Just a little sugar. Thank you."

The two talked for a while about the restaurant and brewery, Lauren and Steven, and even the weather. Jane knew Gabriel wanted to know how she was doing; however, Jane did her best to avoid any conversation about losing Damian's baby and their complicated relationship. She wasn't sure, though, how much longer she would be able to dodge them with Gabriel.

"I wanted to say thank you for coming to the hospital that day. Sorry I couldn't meet you for coffee."

"You're sorry? Why would you think you need to apologize? It was hardly your fault," Gabriel questioned as an image of Jane bent over his knee and her perfectly round ass pink from spanking for unnecessary apologies came to mind. It was a habit he wished to break despite knowing she had done it all her life; it was time it stopped.

Her faced flushed once again, self-conscious of what to say next. "Sorry... Ugh! Never mind." Afraid of repeating something stupid, Jane stared at the floor, unsure of her ability to carry on an intelligent conversation with Gabriel. Why did he intimidate her so? *Ugh! Jane, you know the answer.* She was afraid he would see how much she liked him. It wasn't right for her to feel drawn to a kind soul like Gabriel's when she was dealing with her child's passing. Her child, those words were so foreign to Jane, yet at the same time, so close. She was pregnant, not in the traditional sense, but in one that required a decision of saving her life and taking her baby's; Damian's baby. Jane's remorse and shame stirred every day since being released from the hospital. Damian and his baby were gone, and she was left to deal with the rubble of their relationship on her own. In the end, it didn't really matter. It was done, it happened, end of story.

Gabriel saw Jane's inner torment and guilt as tears tumbled down her cheeks. His heart broke for her. He walked over to where

Jane sat weeping quietly, feeling a need to protect Jane from all the hurt she held inside. He cradled Jane into his safe arms, holding her in silence as she cried. As though Jane heard his heart's desire, she wrapped her arms around his chest and nestled her head into him. There were no words spoken as they sat quietly, holding one another close. For the first time in what seemed like forever, Gabriel felt a sense of inner peace, knowing Jane was safe. He found himself wishing it would never end.

The moment Gabriel took her into his arms, Jane felt seen, heard, and, most of all, cared about. Even if it was only for that moment in time, Jane wished it would never end as echoes of every heartbeat, and the ease of his breath, created a calm within the storm she felt was upon her. He tightened his arms around her, creating a safe haven Jane could stay in for the rest of her life. Despite her years with Damian, she never felt this close to him and couldn't deny being held in Gabriel's arms, tucked in close to his chest, felt like home. She never wanted to leave.

The moment Jane dared to allow herself to enjoy these fleeting moments, thoughts flooded her mind of *you are not his type. You are not good enough.* It was impossible that a man like Gabriel Lockhart would be interested in her, for she was weak and damaged, or at least that was how she viewed herself. All of Jane's inner demons quickly destroyed any sense of security, causing her to withdraw from the sanctuary he provided her.

When Jane left Gabriel's arms, he couldn't help but wonder what was going through her mind to have suddenly disconnected from him. Jane couldn't look at him while she recoiled from his arms as though he had crossed an invisible line or boundary. What suddenly changed? What compelled her to leave his embrace? Deep down, Gabriel knew, but now was not the time to pressure her with questions. Jane needed to grieve the losses she had recently suffered; she just needed some time, and he would be there for her. Instead of burdening Jane to talk, he sat beside her in silence and supported her quietly by just being present.

Chapter 10

Lauren knocked softly on the bedroom door. "Jane? There's coffee if you want some."

Lazily, Jane rolled over in bed tucked under a billowy duvet as the sun caressed her skin through the partially opened blinds. She had to admit the idea of coffee sounded divine. "Ok, be right out," Jane called out from under the warm covers, but another five minutes wrapped safely away from reality wouldn't hurt she thought as she threw the duvet over her head.

A short time later, Jane appeared and poured herself a cup of the heavenly nectar.

"Well, it's about time you got up," Lauren teased with a smirk on her face as Jane curled up in a kitchen chair next to her best friend.

"Ha ha ha, very funny." It felt good to sleep in something other than an uncomfortable hospital bed. Thanks for letting me stay with you while I try to get the shambles of my life together. As Jane took a sip of coffee, she realized hearing herself say those words made her feel like a failure. How would she get her life back together after everything? What was life going to be like with the fallout of her failed relationship with the man Jane believed was her everything? And now she lost something they created together: their baby. How was she supposed to go back to the routine of everyday life, when at that time, it was anything but ordinary or routine?

Lauren watched her friend grow quiet, wondering what she was thinking. "You can stay as long as you need to. Give yourself some time to sort things out. In the meantime, we should go back to the condo and pick up your clothes. You don't have much here."

Jane didn't know what to say at that moment. If she had her way, she would walk away from it all to have one minute of peace from the guilt and sadness she felt all the time, weighing down upon her. "Guess I should, before I have to raid your closet," Jane said with a slight smile.

Lauren enjoyed seeing Jane smile. "I have this afternoon off if you would like to go. Or I could go over myself if you don't feel up to it."

"Damian should be at work, so it would be a good time to go. I would like it if you came with me." As Jane walked down the hall, she felt her friend's eyes upon her, knowing Lauren pitied her. She hated being something to pity.

"Ok, honey, take your time." Lauren softly replied as her heart broke, watching Jane walk down the hall. She seemed so broken, so lost.

As Jane got dressed, her every thought revolved around what she was to do next and how she would settle into her new life. Finding a place to live, moving, buying furniture, and other things seemed like such a daunting task. It made her head spin as she wondered how she would manage everything. Jane sat down on the edge of the bed, her head in her hands as she stared at the floor. How was she to do all of it on her own? Suddenly, Jane's cell phone rang. Little did she know, an unexpected twist of fate answered her call.

"Hello?"

"Hi, Jane, it's Gabriel. I just wanted to see how you are?"

"I'm hanging in there. How are you?" Jane asked.

"Hey Jane," Lauren called as she opened the door, "let's stop and get some groceries on the way back and BBQ tonight. I'm craving steak," Lauren said.

"Sounds like you are busy. I can call back later," Gabriel offered.

"No, Lauren took the day off. We're going to the apartment to get some of my things," Jane said, steering the conversation away from anything heavy as she motioned "two minutes" to her friend.

Lauren nodded and whispered, "sorry," and closed the door.

"Can I help in some way?" he offered.

Jane laughed apprehensively and said, "You don't happen to have a spare place I could call home for a while?"

"What if I said I do? I know of a place you could rent for a reasonable price," he replied.

"I was just kidding," Jane said awkwardly, suddenly feeling embarrassed for sounding desperate.

"I'm serious, Jane. There is a half-duplex about ten mins from the hospital that you could rent for probably around $700 a month. It has two bedrooms, and you'd have the basement as well. I know the landlord and could talk to him if you like?"

Jane didn't know what to say. The rent was too good to be true. "$700?" Jane questioned. "I'm not sure what to say." One minute she felt overwhelmed and lost, while the next, she might actually have a place to live.

It's renovated, painted, and has new carpet and appliances. I think it could be an excellent place for you."

"Seriously? Are you sure?"

"I'll talk to the landlord and will let you know. It is vacant, so you could probably have it anytime."

"I'm not sure what to say. Thank you," Jane stated in disbelief that something was going right for a change.

"Great. I will be in touch later. I better go. I have a meeting in a few minutes. I am happy to help, Jane, anytime," Gabriel said.

"Thank you, Gabriel," she quietly said.

"Jane, try not to stress about things, and just enjoy your day. I'll call you later."

Jane set down her cell and sat there wondering what just occurred. Having a place of her own would be amazing. She didn't want to burden Lauren for long, but she no sooner thought of her friend when Jane heard her speak.

"What did Gabriel want?" Lauren said flatly as she walked into the bedroom.

"He wanted to see how I was and get this: he knows of a half-duplex for rent, and he is going to talk to the landlord for me. It would be great not to have to worry about trying to find a place to live on top of everything," Jane said.

"I see. Well, you can stay here for as long as you want or need to, Jane." Lauren said as she sat beside Jane.

Jane wondered why Lauren was so dismissive of his kind offer. Perhaps she thought Gabriel had an ulterior motive.

Lauren stayed quiet, for she didn't trust Gabriel Lockhart with her friend's well-being. She wasn't sure exactly why she was so uncertain about him, given how he was treating Jane. Maybe it was the fact Jane was so gullible and trusting of him, without a really good reason to be, as they hardly knew one another. But if he could help Jane find a good place to live… She sighed. She would let it go for now. The dark circles under Jane's eyes made it clear to her Jane wasn't sleeping well, and perhaps knowing Gabriel found a good place for her to live would allow her some peace and make her feel less stressed.

"Well," Lauren started to say, then paused, "speaking of moving, we should go over to the condo and get some of your things."

Jane nodded, "I'll be five minutes."

"Ok," said Lauren, smiling.

As Jane got herself ready to go, she began wondering, did Lauren have something against Gabriel? Maybe she disapproved of his help out of loyalty to Brooke. Or perhaps Lauren thought he felt sorry for her. Every time she saw him, it was impossible to meet his gaze, for his dark, mysterious eyes seemed to pierce her soul with one hypnotizing glance. There was no doubt in Jane's mind that Gabriel's eyes could render any female a lusty-filled wanton woman and make them weak in the knees. When he was near, it was like he possessed a gift, making you forget about all your troubles and fears. Gabriel Lockhart was an enchanting cocktail of pure masculine ecstasy, a rare kind of man who was far outside of her reach. Jane caught a glimpse of herself in the mirror and didn't like what she saw, a woman who some might consider pretty but forgettable. With that, she sighed, deciding it was best to focus on what she dreaded most at that moment, going back to her once-upon-a-time home.

Jane's hand trembled as she put the key in the lock of the condo door. Much to her relief, Damian's truck was not parked in the outside stall when they pulled up. She wouldn't have been able to face him, considering how things had ended between them. Despite all of the hurt and pain, Jane couldn't escape the smell of Damian's cologne as they walked into the familiar living room. Jane looked around, noticing it was slightly unkempt with some glasses and beer cans on the coffee table and dirty dishes in the sink and on the counter. With the curtains drawn, darkness gave the place an uninviting and lonely presence. She recalled many nights spent on the sofa, eating take-out and watching movies that often led to them tangled in passion-filled kisses and a fierce embrace. She closed her eyes as the taste of Damian upon her lips took her back in time to when they were happy. She craved his touch upon her naked body, caressing and gentle, as he nibbled and sucked on her until she came many times. The thought brought back echoes of his panting moans as he'd filled her with his cum then lay with his arms wrapped around her, still hard inside her. Jane's eyes welled up with tears; she missed him every day and still loved him, despite the way things ended. Every inch of the apartment claimed a piece of her heart, a place where love used to live and breathe.

Lauren watched her friend fight off tears and felt a small piece of her own heart break at the sight of Jane's look of defeat, surely due to the memories she was no doubt recalling. "I'll go get a couple of suitcases," Lauren said. She understood the amount of loss Jane had gone through shattered her, and she had no idea of how to comfort Jane, leaving her feeling helpless. But not long after, despair turned to anger as hatred for Damian, and the pain he caused her best friend, consumed Lauren's heart. One thing Lauren knew, it was essential to support Jane and her need to start a new life, one on her own.

"What the fuck are you doing here?" Lauren suddenly recognized that voice: Damian. Quickly, she ran to the living room.

"Damian, stop!" Jane tried to say out loud, but she struggled to speak.

Lauren immediately saw red as anger and a need for survival kicked in at the sight of Damian pinning Jane up against a wall by her throat. Her face was turning blue as Jane struggled to get out of his grasp.

"Let her go, asshole!" Lauren screamed as she ran up behind Damian and kicked him between his legs with everything she had. Immediately, Damian let go of Jane just before falling to the floor, yelling in agony. Jane stumbled away from where Damian lay to Lauren's side. She was shaking. Lauren stated, "I'll go get the suitcase; you get outside to the car. I'll meet you there."

Even though Jane heard Lauren's words, her body was frozen in place, unable to move as she coughed and tried to catch her breath.

"Jane! Go!" Lauren yelled demandingly.

It was what Jane needed for her to see the front door, but she realized Damian was lying too close to it. She decided to go through the patio door and knew Lauren would see from the hallway that it was open. She began to walk out onto the patio but then remembered the car was locked, and Lauren's purse was still by the front door. Jane had no choice but to go back inside.

"Lauren!" Jane called out in a panic seeing Damian attacking Lauren as she made her way to the patio door. Jane hesitated a moment so she could come up with a plan of what to do. There wasn't any way she could overpower him; he was far too strong. Jane's focus shifted upon a kitchen chair nearby where she stood. Picking it up, Jane struck the chair over Damian's back, forcing him to let go of Lauren's arm and the suitcase. The two women ran out of the condo to the car, then sped away. Jane and Lauren sat in silence for several blocks before Lauren pulled over. Jane saw her friend shaking, with tears welled up in her eyes and her fingers wrapped around the steering wheel like a vice grip.

"It's ok, Lauren. You are ok." Jane said consolingly, taking her friend's hand in hers. "We are ok. I'm ok. Please, Lauren, look at me," she begged. "I'm ok." Jane's eyes pleaded with her best friend to see for herself and to know they were safe.

Lauren looked at her friend and wondered how she did it. How did Jane push through her own fear to comfort her? Lauren glanced back at Jane, squeezing Jane's hand tightly as she realized something: Jane was so strong. In fact, she was stronger and more resilient than anyone else she knew. What had happened to Jane for her to possess the ability to handle so many hardships in her life? Overwhelmed by her friend's caring heart, Lauren wiped her tears away and smiled at Jane, then asked, "What? It's just allergies."

Jane smiled, feeling relieved Lauren trusted her enough to listen and understand that they were safe.

Despite the strength Jane exhibited, there lay a nagging guilty feeling in the back of her mind as Jane knew if they hadn't gone over to the condo, Damian would never have attacked Lauren. It made Jane sick to her stomach to think of what he would have done to her. It was all her fault. Jane's mind wouldn't let go of the what-if scenarios riddling her with guilt and shame as she turned her gaze out the window hoping Lauren wouldn't see the tears welled up in her eyes. Her best friend could have been seriously hurt! Everything was beginning to spin out of control, and waves of nausea hit Jane like a ton of bricks. She was going to be sick, and the chokehold of guilt made it near impossible for Jane to breathe.

"Lauren, can you please pull over?" Jane pleaded.

Lauren realized Jane was struggling and quickly pulled the car into a nearby parking lot. Swiftly, Jane got out of the car and dropped to her knees, dry heaving, with gasping breaths.

"Slow deep breaths," Lauren said to her and massaged Jane's shoulders. "Come on, Jane, breathe with me."

Rooted deep within her soul, Jane vowed she would never again allow Damian to hurt her best friend. She had no idea how, but one way or another, she would ensure her safety.

"Come on, let's go home," Lauren said, assisting Jane to her feet.

Chapter 11

"Welcome back," an enthusiastic Justin said as Jane approached the security desk. "Didn't know you were coming back today!"

"Thanks," she said with a slight smile. "Justin, I haven't been able to thank you for helping me."

Justin seemed quietly proud of himself and relished Jane's appreciation. "I'm just happy you are here, and you look great!" He walked towards Jane with extended arms. "How are you doing?"

Jane realized he was going to give her a hug but silently wished he wouldn't. As Justin wrapped his arms around her, Jane felt awkward and uncomfortable feeling his embrace. Her body stiffened, and she didn't return his hug. "I'm doing well," Jane said back, ensuring she didn't promote any interest in his gesture.

"That's great to hear," he said as he stepped back from Jane. "Well, I suppose I should let you go to work." Justin winked and smiled.

Jane couldn't help but notice he brushed his hand against hers before walking back to the security desk.

"Catch you later," he said over his shoulder.

Jane walked onto the elevator and pushed the fourth-floor button, thinking how strange it was to be back in the same place where she lost something precious. With every floor that passed by on the panel display, Jane wondered how everyone would behave around her. The last thing she wanted to see was pity on their faces as they constantly asked how she was doing. "Just breathe," Jane quietly whispered to herself as the doors of the elevator opened, and she took the first few steps onto the unit. As she walked towards the staff room, a few familiar faces greeted her with smiles and well wishes. *So far, so good. Maybe today will be ok.* Jane pushed open the staff room door and was utterly overwhelmed by the loud, enthusiastic applause from her co-workers. She wasn't sure if it was the jarring surprise of cheers or perhaps the fleeting hope she had for an ordinary day that made Jane tear up. She smiled and dabbed the tears at the corner of her eyes before she embarrassed herself further.

"We're so happy you're back, Jane!" her manager said.

Jane smiled and in a soft voice, said, "Thank you." It felt good to be back rather than dwelling upon her messed up life, and she had to admit, she secretly hoped to avoid anyone asking her what happened and all the drama she presumed the staff gossiped about. Jane dreaded answering questions in fear of everyone thinking she was a disaster. Despite everyone's joyful welcome, Jane desperately wanted to go back to work, blend in, and forget about her fractured soul.

Much to her relief, the day flew by. Not long after her last break, Jane nestled within a small group of people in the elevator, set to leave for the day. She looked forward to feeling the sun's rays on her face as she walked to the staff parking lot. A sense of gratitude washed over her as she reminisced over the day and how no one inquired about the recent tragic event. Perhaps it was out of respect or whatever the management team told them, but she was grateful regardless. However, even though her heart felt a sense of peace, Jane wished her feet felt the same. She clearly had been away long enough for her body to forget what it was like to be on her feet all day. Looking down, Jane found her runner lace undone and knelt to tie it.

"Jane! Hey, wait up," a male voice called out behind her.

As she tried to see who called out to her, Jane stood up quickly with her shoe in hand.

"Here, let me help." a stern yet concerned voice said, and a hand extended for her to take. It was Justin, and he didn't come empty-handed. He cradled in his arm a beautiful bouquet of assorted fragrant flowers wrapped in rustic brown and paper tied with a pretty bow.

Jane couldn't help but smile. They were beautiful. "I dare say, someone is very lucky to be getting such a gift."

"Here," Justin held out a free hand for Jane to steady herself with while she stood up. Shyly, Jane looked at Justin and said, "Thank you."

"Well, they are for a woman who happens to be very lucky," he said, smiling as he handed the stunning bouquet to Jane, keeping her hand in his.

Jane's cheeks flushed a similar bright pink shade as some of the flowers rendered her tongue-tied. All she could do was look to the ground and say, "Thank you, they're beautiful." At the touch of his hand in hers, Jane was confused about his intention, causing her to quickly pull it away.

"I was wondering if you might like to go out sometime?" Justin politely asked.

Caught off guard, Jane wasn't sure what to do with his forwardness. He never expressed any interest in meeting outside of work before, and she wasn't sure what to feel or think and had zero idea what to say back in that moment. Justin was a co-worker, not someone whom she thought of as a friend, and certainly not in any way romantically. What was she going to do now?

Justin saw Jane's cheeks flush and a sense of pride came over him. He decided to take advantage of that moment and leaned in and whispered into her ear, "I like you, Jane." Then he gave her a quick sweet kiss on her cheek.

Jane had no idea of what she honestly felt. He was very kind and had always treated her well, and with that thought in the back of her mind, letting her guard down slightly, Jane smiled back to him. "Thank you. Maybe we could do coffee one afternoon?" she proposed. Coffee was always a safe option, and they could do it at work; well, that was her plan anyway.

"Great! It's a date." Justin exclaimed. He knew he would have to work slowly on Jane, given her recent relationship woes. He would be patient with her; she was worth it. Grinning widely, Justin found it challenging to hold back his joy. "Here is my cell number. Text me when you have a chance, and we can set something up." He handed her a business card with his number on it before he turned and started to walk back to the hospital, leaving Jane to sort out what just happened. She wondered what she agreed to as she looked down at the card in one hand and the flowers in the other.

She needed to talk to Lauren and immediately called her cell number. Jane couldn't stop shaking. Why would she be shaking like a leaf? What was happening to her? A moment later, Jane recognized that feeling which had plagued her the last few minutes: regret. How she wished she could turn back time and tell Justin she wasn't interested in going out with him. He was friendly, but she didn't want to date him, and she certainly didn't need any trouble at work. God knows, Jane had had her fair share of issues with boyfriends and desired to be on her own for a while. "Damn!" Voicemail. "Hey, Lauren, it's Jane. I'll pick up Chinese on my way home. We need to talk."

"So, he just came up to you, told you were beautiful, kissed your cheek, and handed you the flowers?" Lauren quizzed as she took a mouthful of Chinese food with a mystified look upon her face.

"Yes, and he asked me out! All I could do was stand there and nod, and then I realized what I had agreed to. I don't know, Lauren. I don't want to go out with him. What am I supposed to do now?" Jane sighed as she took a sip of wine.

"Why don't you want to go out with him? Are you afraid? Not everyone is Damian, Jane, and not to mention he saved your life once. Doesn't that count for something?" Lauren quizzed.

How could Jane forget that little bit of headline news? The problem was, Jane didn't know why she didn't want to go out with him. "You know when there is just something, but you can't put your finger on it? That's how I feel about Justin; I don't know."

Lauren looked at Jane and saw the worry on her best friend's pretty face, but she had no clue what to tell her. Why was Jane so bothered by Justin asking her out? What was it about Justin that troubled Jane or made her feel uncomfortable? Lauren wasn't sure what to think but thought it was best to let it go, at least for now.

The day had been long, and soon the two friends said good night. Jane sat on her bed and looked out to the dark sky while the moonlight cast shadows about her room. She looked at the clock: 22:22 hrs. Ugh, Jane thought to herself. She couldn't turn her mind off, longing for the days when life wasn't so challenging. Why was her life so complicated? It all seemed to unravel when she and Damian broke up, and as Jane thought more about it, she wondered why. Despite talking with Lauren, Jane was no closer to understanding what was next or how to get there, other than knowing she didn't want to go on a date with Justin.

She succumbed to the fact that she wasn't about to get any sleep, so perhaps some tea would relax her mind and body. While waiting for the kettle to boil, Jane stared out the kitchen window. She felt compelled to enjoy her tea on the porch wrapped up in a blanket, as it was a lovely, mostly warmish night. As she sat sipping her tea with the tranquil company of the moon, Jane's mind returned to a common theme in her life, all the men: Damian, Gabriel, and now Justin. It almost seemed like a soap opera to her, but she had to find a way to let Damian go, sort out her feelings for Gabriel, and try to get out of her date with Justin. Jane exhaled a long sigh as she looked up to the nearly full moon.

One thought came to mind: she hadn't heard from Gabriel since she agreed to take the apartment, and she wondered if she should message him. Would it seem desperate if she did, or would he perceive her as being a bother? Gabriel was the only man she felt like herself with, where she didn't have to pretend to be something she wasn't. The only problem was her inability to disguise her interest in him. She wasn't exactly trusting of herself as of late. But she never felt pressured around him, which may be the reason she enjoyed talking with him. Talking felt easy, not forced, which made her feel more confident. He always lent his ear and offered some honest and wise solutions, which she greatly appreciated. Things didn't seem so difficult after she talked with Gabriel.

Enjoying the peaceful night, wrapped up in a cozy blanket on a lounge chair, Jane's solitude was interrupted by a rustling sound nearby. She looked out over the front yard and couldn't see anything in the light cast by the street lights. Pulling her blanket closer around her, Jane walked to the end of the front steps and peered over to the bushes separating Lauren's property from the neighbour's, but nothing caught her eye. Dismissing the noise as a cat out prowling around, Jane turned to go back to the chair when something moved in the darkness, catching her eye. And it was definitely larger than a cat.

With her heart racing, Jane called out, "Is anyone there?" But no one replied, not that she had expected them to. She suddenly realized she wasn't alone. "Shit," Jane said quietly to herself as she saw the orange glow of what Jane believed was a cigarette; someone was definitely out there watching her. Scared, Jane ran into the house, found her cell phone, and dialed 911 as quickly as her nervous fingers would allow. Was it some kid up to no good, or was it…? Jane's mind paused in thought, was it possible? Damian used to smoke when they dated, but he quit when they began living together. She'd noticed he pulled out a package of cigarettes one night when he was leaving to go hang out with the guys, but she didn't ask him in fear it would cause an argument. Was it Damian in the bushes watching her? But why would he?

A 911 dispatcher suddenly came on the line, and Jane gave all of the information she could. He asked if she could still see the person, but she no longer saw the orange glow of the cigarette and didn't see the shadow-like figure any longer. Her fear had swiftly escalated to DEFCON 1. The dispatcher's encouragement helped Jane feel less alone, and he offered to stay on the line with her until the police arrived. She hoped there wouldn't be much noise, as waking up Lauren and causing her to worry was the last thing she wanted to do. Deep down, Jane knew someone was watching her, and it scared her to death.

"Oh, no! I can see the orange glow again," Jane exclaimed to the dispatcher, whispering loudly as the fear rose within her stomach.

The dispatcher encouraged Jane to stay inside, where she was safe, and told her that the police were only a couple of minutes away. He also asked her to describe the person if Jane could see them. But Jane still could not see anything besides a dark figure and the occasional draw of the cigarette.

Moments later, the police arrived, parking their cars a few houses down. A feeling of instant relief washed over Jane. With their flashlights, the police searched the areas between both homes on either side of Lauren's and the backyards and alley, but they found nothing except the few cigarette butts left behind where the person stood watching. From that area, the front porch was in full view, making Jane shudder at the idea of how she'd felt so safe not so long ago. The police met Jane outside and explained what they had found and got a statement from her. Unfortunately, there was not much for them to go on, nor was there any visual to get some idea about whether the person was male or female. The kind officers ensured Jane there was no one in the immediate area and gave her a business card to contact them if she had any questions or remembered any details later. Despite them doing a thorough search and offering to patrol the area tonight, Jane admitted that the idea of someone lurking in the shadows made her skin crawl.

Jane decided not to worry Lauren by waking her up and would tell her another time. She knew Lauren would be upset, but there wasn't anything to go on, so no point worrying her too.

A few blocks away, a person got into a truck and lit another cigarette, thinking *that was a close call but worth it.* Seeing Jane, and how peaceful she looked while sitting on the porch had them wishing to be near her. Their interest in what happened after they left the scene had them wondering, so they drove near the residence and saw the lights on despite it being midnight. They recalled how earlier, the two friends had eaten as they sat in the living room, talking and laughing, and they wondered what their conversations were like, but with the windows closed, details of what the friends talked about would remain a mystery. But then, much to their surprise and delight, Jane had walked onto the front porch wrapped in a blanket and holding a cup of tea. She sat in the lounger and made herself comfortable. The temptation to stay and watch her was too much to pass up, and they had observed how peaceful she looked while admiring the full moon. That was until she realized she was not alone and ran into the house to call 911. If it hadn't been for the cigarette, they would have been able to enjoy more time together. Perhaps next time. With that thought in mind, they drove off, flicking the butt of their cigarette out the window. In the rearview mirror was the view of the police looking around the property with their flashlights.

Chapter 12

Moving day! Jane woke that morning and felt both excitement and trepidation as she realized today was the start of a new life on her terms. She should have been excited and maybe even filled with nervous anticipation, but this morning, Jane woke up feeling worried. Since that night she called the police when she realized someone was watching her; Jane could not shake off the feeling that someone was always near, that someone was still watching her. But the idea of hiding at Lauren's and having Lauren feel like she needed to watch over her was something Jane couldn't take any longer. It was time to leave the familiar security of her friend's home; Jane just hoped there was something concrete to land on after leaping out on her own.

Jane stood outside as the movers did the work to move what little belongings she had taken from the old condo. A sense of gratitude, or maybe an epiphany of sorts, washed over her at the realization that she was free to live a life of her choosing. But how would she know what that was? All Jane ever knew or wanted was to be with Damian, and now that he was gone, what would her life be like without a man by her side? She had never really lived on her own before. There were always roommates, and then Damian, once she graduated from university.

"Miss? Excuse me, Miss?" was all Jane heard, snapping her out of the daydream-like state.

"Yes?" Jane replied, realizing one of the movers was standing near her.

"We are done loading the truck. I just wanted to confirm the address we are going to."

Jane looked at the paperwork and initialled beside the address.

The mover nodded, walked towards the moving truck, and that was it. Jane's entire life was packed onto a truck to be moved to the place she would soon call home. Looking down at the keys to her new place, Jane took a deep breath and walked towards her car. During the drive to her new home, Jane recalled the day Gabriel showed her the place.

"This place is great! Thank you for talking to the landlord for me. I really appreciate it," Jane said as she turned to face Gabriel. She realized he was looking at her, and it sent a wave of heat through her body, which, without a doubt, didn't go unnoticed by him. Jane had no idea what to say, feeling awkward and unsure of herself; she decided to walk towards the kitchen in the hope of creating some distance from him, buying some time to collect herself.

Gabriel admitted to himself that he revelled in the idea she was smitten with him, and he enjoyed seeing the pretty pink glow of her cheeks. He had no intention of letting Jane leave him feeling shameful, as she had nothing to feel embarrassed about. "It is a great place, and the neighbour next door is not a problem; she has been living there for about six years, and she is very nice, from what I understand."

"That's reassuring to hear." Jane couldn't be more thankful for a place to call her own, and even more so of Gabriel's help. She felt relieved she didn't have to do the search completely on her own, a task she viewed as daunting, leaving her to feel somewhat lost of where to even begin. But in the end, she knew this place was the best option for her, and in that moment, Jane turned to Gabriel and stated, "I'll take it!" She had a new home, a second chance, a place to feel safe.

Gabriel handed Jane an envelope. "Here is the lease agreement. Take a look over it, and I can swing by and pick it up after you've signed it. If you have any questions, please call me anytime."

"Thanks." Curious as to why he was the person to call instead of the landlord, Jane opened the envelope and quickly glanced over it. No sign of a landlord's name. *Weird.* Nervously, Jane wondered if she was doing the right thing. She glanced over the agreement and saw the amount of rent due each month, and it was something Jane knew she could handle on her own. Being able to curl up on the couch and fall asleep without someone wondering if she was ok all the time made her decision to sign the agreement less intimidating, and somehow Jane knew it was a good thing.

As Jane read over the lease agreement, Gabriel studied her pretty face and wondered what had happened between her and Damian, as Jane had not confided in him at all about the couple's recent challenges. Deciding it was worth the risk of asking, Gabriel said, "Jane, I realize you and Damian broke up a while ago. Is it possible things could be worked out between you both?"

Gabriel's question caught her off guard, causing her to stumble over her words. "We… um… he left. We broke up because he wanted to be with another woman." Immediately, Jane felt ashamed, staring down at the floor, unable to hide from Gabriel. How she wished people would stop asking her about Damian. He wasn't the man she believed him to be, and she was a fool for thinking they had a future together. She was a gullible fool.

It was then Gabriel understood why she hesitated to say anything about their breakup. Undoubtedly, Jane blamed herself for the affair, but she endured the most terrible loss of Damian's baby on top of everything else. Jane needed time to heal, which will be both challenging and painful, but Gabriel secretly promised her he would do his best to protect her and give whatever time she needed to heal her wounded heart.

Silently, Jane walked towards Gabriel with the signed lease in hand. She couldn't look at him, feeling insecure and defeated. He was a successful businessman, and she was a woman who relied upon the generosity of a landlord who clearly rented to her at a discounted amount, indeed out of pity, Jane concluded in her mind. Without Gabriel's help, she couldn't help but wonder what the rent would have been or if she would have been able to find such a great place to live on her own.

"Well, that was fast," Gabriel said teasingly. "You can take some more time if you would like."

"No, I am good. I don't want to lose this place; it's great."

"Ok then!" He smiled. "Here are the keys. Welcome to your new home, Jane."

His smile made Jane's heart race and butterflies flutter in her stomach. She couldn't let on to Gabriel any hint of her foolish crush; he was far too intelligent, handsome, and way out of her league.

"Congratulations, Jane. I'm delighted you are living here and can start fresh. When you have an idea of when you are moving in, let me know, and I can help you move in.

Shyly, Jane said, "Thanks. Not sure how much I will have to move." Just hearing those words made Jane feel less in every way: a failure in her relationships, a failure in having a home of her own, and a failure in filling a home with love. To make matters worse, she stood in the presence of a man who was not only successful in every way but also who lived a very comfortable life in a beautiful home, she was sure. Jane suddenly felt incredibly uneasy and turned away from Gabriel.

Gabriel saw the familiar disgraceful look upon Jane's pretty face and wondered what she was thinking about to have her look so defeated. Instinctively, he took a step towards her; however, Jane defensively stepped back from his advance, and he paused his need to comfort Jane without putting any uneasy pressure upon her. Stepping back, Gabriel decided it was best if he left. "I should get going back to the brewery. Let me know when you are set to move, and I will be there for you."

Jane nodded. "Thank you again," she said. After he left, Jane stood at the front door, feeling a mix of emotions: happy she had a place to live on her own again and somewhat melancholy as she stood alone in the empty condo. Everything that had happened to her over the last few months made her wonder if life was going to work out for her. Was her life ever going to feel happy again?

"Excuse me, Miss? Miss?" Jane heard a man say her name, snapping her back to reality. She saw one of the mover's quizzical faces and realized she had zoned out, almost forgetting where she was for a brief moment, suddenly realizing it was the day she was moving.

"I'm sorry. I… what was your question?" Jane asked the young man.

"I just wasn't sure where this chair goes," he said.

"Oh, that can go into the master bedroom. Thank you," Jane said quickly. Good Lord, she had to keep her head about her. Daydreaming was not an option. "Get it together, Jane," she quietly scolded herself.

A few hours later, the movers left, and Jane was surrounded by boxes labelled for every room, which served as a reminder to her of what exactly life had all come down to. A woman who had lost everything she ever wanted and loved. Tears misted over Jane's eyes as the sudden weight of her crumbled world crashed down around her. Jane slowly sat down on the floor in the middle of the living room while the evening sun cast a shadow over the room. Looking around her, Jane thought about what her life had become and remembered Damian's last words to her. "I don't love you anymore. You are a prude. You make me sick," echoed like a never-ending nightmare in her thoughts. Sobs filled her chest, and tears streamed down her cheeks as every unkind word he hissed in anger seared her heart again, leaving Jane feeling defeated and broken. So much change and sorrow, how was she going to go on? How was she to get through every day, every minute? How?! Exhaustion compelled Jane to lie down on the floor, where she quietly sobbed, wondering when life would feel less complicated. She slowly drifted to sleep, surrounded by boxes filled with all the tokens and fragments of her once-upon-a-time happy life.

Hours later, Jane woke up feeling stiff and a bit sore, struggling to recall where she was in her unfamiliar surroundings and on the floor. With every blink feeling like her eyes were like sandpaper, Jane looked at her watch to see it was 2:42 a.m. As Jane looked about her, she remembered the previous long day of moving. Jane got herself up and sat down on a nearby chair.

Every box held a piece of her life, of which she had no idea what to do with. The emptiness of her new home seemed like a lot of space to fill on her own. Would she like living there? Looking around her, Jane noticed a box labelled pictures, which caused an unbearable agony of what felt like a million tiny cuts as she felt compelled to open it against her better judgement. Sifting through the endless memories, Jane found a picture of her and Damian framed in wood with carvings of seashells taken while away on a Mexican beach vacation. They looked happy. Their smiles showed a couple who were in love and couldn't keep their hands off one another. Jane remembered that they'd found a quiet, secluded part of the beach that day. Damian had pulled out his cell phone and wrapped her in his arms while Jane turned and kissed his cheek just as Damian had taken the picture. His eyes showed the joy he felt, and she realized she did make him happy once, but then everything changed. What or why? Jane wasn't sure. One day they were content and madly in love, unable to keep their hands off one another, and then, they were not. Jane felt empty and hollow and her hands began to shake as her heart took over, making it nearly impossible not to be swallowed up by the sorrow. It was all too much to handle. Jane perilously wanted her old life back. She wanted to be loved, to be seen, to matter to someone who cared about her. How would she manage on her own? Would she ever feel whole again and not the wounded stray who wasn't wanted by anyone? Feeling tired, Jane soon found herself blanketed in the soft glow of the moon's light, comforting her to sleep as she curled up on the sofa.

It was so bright, Jane thought to herself when she suddenly realized she was not in bed but on the couch, enclosed by several boxes. Attempting to open her eyes but blinded by the bright sun's rays, Jane quickly closed them. Where was she? Why did she feel so tired? As she sat up and looked around, Jane remembered the move. A heavy sigh left her chest as she thought about all of the unpacking to be done. Guess there was no time like the present.

Several hours later, Jane sat down with warm tea after a long day of unpacking all of the boxes in the hopes of making the new place feel more like home. She missed the beautiful sunny day and wasn't wanting to miss out on the warm night. She stepped out onto the front doorstep. A clear starry night sky made Jane feel relaxed, and she smiled to herself, realizing she was home. Despite her misleading fears deep down, Jane took in a few cleansing deep breaths, then slowly exhaled, letting in the appreciation of that moment. She released her sorrow the night before, as difficult as it was, and Jane concluded she would be ok. With some time, her heart and head would believe and feel the same way; it would just take some time.

They watched Jane sit quietly on the front step, admiring how she looked with her hair in a messy bun, wearing sweat pants, a hoody, and no makeup; she looked beautiful. But her life was not complete being single and on her own. They believed they could fulfill her needs and desperately wanted to be that person for her. Knowing where Jane now lived, they would ensure she was safe and taken care of. After taking one last drag of a cigarette, they casually tossed it out the window. Tomorrow, they would return and watch from afar and would do so every night until she was theirs.

Chapter 13

Brooke boarded the plane and found her first-class seat. It had been a few weeks since she started her new position in London, but she needed to return to the US for some business at the San Fransisco office. Even though the two friends had talked once a week since she left, Brooke wanted to surprise Lauren with an impromptu visit, so she didn't mention the trip during their last conversation. The flight was long, even as Brooke did some work. Taking a break, she looked out the window at the billowy, cloud-covered view below them and the bright blue sky above, where she couldn't help but wonder how Gabriel was. She had talked with Lauren extensively about their break up, and since her move, Brooke still pondered if she made the right decision.

She recalled the last time she and Gabriel were together before things changed so drastically between them. Although they mutually agreed to split up and part as friends, Brooke, as of late, wondered if there was a possibility she could run into him during this visit. Was Gabriel single or perhaps dating other women? Was he with Jane? God, she hoped not.

Brooke wasn't sure what to expect should they run into one another; however, the idea of Gabriel being with Jane made her feel sick to her stomach. She fidgeted in her seat as the unrelenting taunting of Gabriel being with Jane spun about in her mind. Brooke took a sip of wine, and memories of the last time she and

Gabriel were together surfaced as she gazed at the dreamy heaven-like scenery.

"Come to bed," Brooke smiled coyly at Gabriel, pulling the covers back.

Gabriel walked towards the bed, his eyes never letting go of Brooke's gaze, as an animalistic need to take her swelled deep within him. His muscles tensed with anticipation as lust coursed through his heart, feeding his desire like kindling to a fire. Gabriel removed his T-shirt before crawling across the bed and stopping as he hovered over Brooke. His dark eyes penetrated through to her soul, she believed, while shivers cascaded over her body. "You dressed up," he teased with admiration of the emerald green babydoll set with a front tie provocatively teasing him to tug at the silken ribbon.

Brooke tousled her long, dark hair, her eyes locking on Gabriel, wonderstruck by what he was about to do. "Do you like what you see?" she cooed.

"Mmm, very much so," Gabriel stated with a sultry smile, straddling Brooke's hips, reaching out, taking hold of both of her wrists, and holding them together with one hand above her head. With his free hand, he guided Brooke to turn her head slightly before leaning in close, whispering in her ear, "I want you."

Immediately, Brooke's body felt the weight of Gabriel's upon her, forcing her to move as he wanted, unable to escape his grasp. She had never had a boyfriend as dominant as Gabriel, and she wasn't sure if she enjoyed the lack of control. Her body responded with insatiable needy lust, despite her wishing she could free herself from his grip, as she craved to wrap her arms around him, touch him, and let him know she wanted him just as much. But it was no use. He was far too strong despite her struggles, which increased the anxious feeling rising within her. His strength was undeniable, causing Brooke to feel perplexed. Did she like it? Or was she threatened by the lack of control, pulling once again to free her hands in a futile effort?

"What's wrong? Feeling trapped? Gabriel questioned teasingly, kissing along the length of her elegant neck, taking great pleasure in relishing her scent and body.

The truth was, Brooke found it difficult to focus upon the pleasure he bestowed upon her while her mind wrestled with being unable to free herself. Why was she fighting it so much? Any woman whose body was being deliciously relished by a man, who was safe and sane, would be putty in his hands. Why could she not relax and enjoy the sensations and just let go? She was too present in her head, ignoring the instincts of her body or heart? Knowing she mattered and felt seen, lusted after, and loved was what every woman's heart and soul yearned for. Why was she so different? Why couldn't she accept Gabriel's heart?

Gabriel felt the uncomfortable tension in Brooke's body and decided it was best to let go of her wrists and lie down beside her. His hand gently caressed her arm as the two lay in silence, and he quietly watched Brooke, curious of what she was thinking. "What are you thinking? Are you upset with me?"

Hesitating to find her words, Brooke wasn't exactly sure what to say, as she had no idea why she couldn't relax and just enjoy their time together. "I don't know," she said, sighing. "I want to, but I just can't." Brooke turned to face Gabriel and gently placed a hand along the side of his face. She searched his eyes for any sign of what he was thinking, but all she saw was a tenderness that melted her heart. Rather than attempting to explain anything, Brooke leaned in close to Gabriel's chest and placed a single kiss upon his lips, hoping he would let it go and they could enjoy one another.

Whatever preoccupied Brooke's mind troubled Gabriel, but he knew pushing her to talk would only end in an argument accomplishing nothing. But deep down, he knew something was up, and he wished she would reconsider not talking about it. The light touch of her hand against his cheek showed such tenderness and femininity as she kissed him. He couldn't help but wonder if she did love him or if finding someone who would not only be a companion but a lover was a fleeting desire. Was she capable of showing her vulnerability to him, building a mutual trust needed between intimate partners? Part of him already knew the answer; however, there remained the slightest hope she would be what he longed for. His body needed to feel close to the exquisite woman lying next to him; he needed her.

Gabriel wontedly gazed at Brooke, urging her to move closer to the gorgeous man who lay beside her. His intense, smouldering eyes gave away the secret his body held onto, making it near impossible for Brooke to ignore. Leaning in close, she passionately kissed his lips, teasing with her tongue and gently taking his lower lip between her teeth. The carnal desire was evident between them both, but neither one felt any need to rush and instead chose to savour one another, be present, and let their misgivings and inhibitions go, even for just a few moments.

"I need you now," she whispered against Gabriel's lips.

"Mmm, I like the sound of that. Now, if we only could do something about you still wearing that inviting..." One small tug of the ribbon tie, "sexy..." Another pull, "enchanting teddy you are still wearing." With one last seductive pull on the ribbon, Gabriel teased with a sexy smile but then stopped. He felt like a kid at Christmas opening a gift and wanted to savour the sight of Brooke for a moment.

But Brooke wasn't nearly as patient. "I might need some help," she coyly smiled while she straddled Gabriel's hips. The craving to feel his hardness against her throbbing wetness drove her crazy with fervour, evident from her soaked thong. As Brooke looked at Gabriel, her eyes drank in the contours of his broad shoulders and lingered upon his chiselled chest while her inner vixen yearned to come out and play.

"I love touching you," Brooke cooed as she teasingly traced a finger across Gabriel's chest slowly towards his shoulder and down to his hand. "I need your help."

Gabriel smiled, "Oh? What can I help you with?" Intrigued, Gabriel wondered what she had in mind behind her mischievous smile.

"Can I have your hands?"

"And what would you like my hands to do?" Gabriel asked, intently gazing at Brooke.

"I need you to finish untying the ribbon." Brooke slyly smiled. The feeling of the satin material, which delectably covered Brooke's sumptuous breasts, made it nearly impossible for him not to indulge in his yearning to touch her. Without saying a word, he ran a finger over her breast's perfectly contoured curve. Her skin felt like velvet under his touch. As he traced her exposed skin, the other hand slowly pulled on an end of the ribbon one last time, releasing it.

Brooke looked intensely into Gabriel's eyes, waiting with great anticipation for what was to come next. The ribbon fell to her side. Gabriel waited a moment, seeing Brooke's breathing go shallow as her excitement had become harder to resist. Impatiently, she moved to remove the clothing, but Gabriel caught her wrist, commanding, "No, that's my job." Brooke froze, unsure of what to do. She knew he liked to do things his way, but tonight, she had no idea how to anticipate what or how that was.

Gabriel saw the look of confusion on her face and decided to make it known just how much he desired her. In a swift move, he sat up, sliding the satin material down Brooke's arms, tying the ribbon around her wrists in front of her, and leaving her exposed for his pleasure and soon for hers.

Brooke's heart skipped a few beats. She felt vulnerable and exposed and wasn't sure she liked it. But for the sake of her relationship, Brooke decided to go with it and see if she would enjoy it this one time.

"What...," was all Brooke could manage to say before Gabriel's hand fisted the back of her hair, and his teeth gently tugged at her lower lip. His eyes intently captured Brooke's as he let her lip slide from his hold, and she winced slightly. She had great lips, full, supple, and perfect for kissing. He pulled her closer to his body as their lips met, and her sweet scent and taste filled his senses. Their tongues entwined, his breath became hers, and soon the world around them disappeared as ecstasy took over. Knowing Brooke was unable to move as he held her firmly against his chest, his hand in her hair, he devoured her lips with his for several minutes. Brooke remained straddled over Gabriel's hips, enabling him to touch between her legs with ease, "Mmm, someone's excited," he teased. Her wetness soaked through the satin of her thong, enticing him to delve deeper.

Brooke's head fell back into his hand, and she moaned softly as she relaxed, enjoying the feeling of his finger inside her thong smoothly sliding deep inside her wetness. Her moans were evidence of the pleasure she felt while his finger stroked her G-spot and the heel of his hand massaged her swollen mound.

"Oh God," Brooke huskily whispered as Gabriel encouraged her to lift her lips to his. Her need to cum quickly rose, and she felt the need to pull away to catch her breath. Brooke looked deeply into his eyes, but there were no words, only the intense synergy between them that seemed to penetrate Brooke's soul.

"I need to cum," she whispered between breaths. "I can't wait."

"You want to cum? What do you say?" Gabriel mused, placing a kiss upon Brooke's seductively parted lips, watching how her eyes dilated as he kept her teetering on the edge of ecstasy with his hand between her legs. Knowing she would spill over at the slightest change of his touch fed his dominant ego, knowing her pleasure was at his will. "Do you want to cum, Brooke? Tell me," he commanded.

Brooke quickly replied, panting, "Yes." A salacious hunger stirred her feminine need, edging her body into a sinful frenzy. Despite not being able to use her hands, Brooke knew his need to fuck her was equally as fierce, and she couldn't wait, but he knew exactly what he was doing, and it drove her insane. His need to hear her beg to cum irritated her so. "Just do it already," she demanded, having had enough of this game.

Brooke's body began to quiver heatedly as Gabriel expertly, with ease, brought her body to Nirvana. Her head fell back as her moans filled the room, her body riding the cascading waves of euphoria that crashed down upon her. A few precious moments later, she relaxed, collapsing against Gabriel's chest, panting to catch her breath. Brooke enjoyed the electric pulse surging through her body until she felt her body being lifted and swiftly placed on her back in bed.

The hardness of his cock and the pressure he felt against his jeans became unbearable, craving to be released. Pulling Brooke's body to the edge of the bed, he slid her thong to the side, then with one thrust, buried himself deep inside the warm, cum-filled wetness of her pussy. He paused, savouring the delicious sensations of her wrapped around him, as his own breath quickened with anticipation. He needed to cum, to fill her, to take her. He pulled himself until he was almost free from Brooke's pussy. Gabriel thrust one more time, burying himself to the hilt as the throbbing had become unbearable. Taking hold of Brooke's hips, he ardently fucked her deeply, watching her full breasts bounce in rhythm with each thrust. Brooke's moans grew louder as he rapidly approached a carnal release. His balls swelled with a relentless urge to release his seed. It would be happening soon. The echoes of his thighs slapping up against her peach-like ass spurred his desire to penetrate himself deeper.

Brooke reached down with her tied wrists and, with her fingers, rubbed her clit vigorously. The very sight of her touching herself, pleasuring herself to the point of orgasm, then hearing her wails pushed Gabriel over the edge with ease, to an orgasm so intense he felt he might be unable to stand while his body erupted. He filled Brooke's pussy with his warm cum, making himself quiver. With panting breaths and feeling drained, literally, Gabriel collapsed beside Brooke's used body.

"Miss, would you like another drink?" Brooke heard a flight attendant ask, jolting her from her luscious daydream.

"Coffee with cream, please," Brooke said with her face slightly turned away, hiding her flushed appearance she knew would not go unnoticed.

As Brooke stared out of the window of the plane, she pondered the idea of seeing Gabriel. Would he be willing to see her? Or was he with Jane? Her thong was drenched, and an uncomfortable throbbing between her legs made Brooke shift in her seat. It had been a few months since their last night together. Maybe he would fuck her for old time's sake, even though they didn't talk often. It was doubtful, given the kind of man he was, but still, she wondered, hoping he was doing well and secretly hoping there wasn't anyone special in his life, especially Jane.

Chapter 14

"Oh my god! What are you doing here?" Lauren squealed with excitement upon opening the front door to find a surprise standing in front of her. "I can't believe you are here!" she said as she hugged Brooke tightly.

"I flew back for some business meetings and thought it would be fun to surprise you." Brooke smiled widely, hugging her friend back just as tight.

"I'm so happy you're here! You have to stay with me so we can catch up."

"I have a hotel room booked," Brooke began to say but paused as she saw the look of disapproval upon Lauren's face. "It would be great to visit instead of staying in a hotel room on my own."

"Perfect!" Lauren excitedly exclaimed. "Let's get you a glass of wine." Brooke took a seat in the living room while Lauren came from the kitchen holding a glass of burgundy deliciousness. Casually, she sat in a chair next to the sofa and said, "Jane is coming over tonight for dinner; she'll be so surprised to see you too!"

Upon hearing Jane's name, Brooke immediately felt her pulse race and her blood simmer. "Jane is going to be here?" Brooke asked, trying to sound interested despite her real feelings.

"Yeah, we were going to go over some of the wedding details and have pizza for dinner. She'll be here at six.

"I don't know, Lauren. I have a hotel room booked, and you two can talk about wedding plans. We can catch up later."

Lauren searched her friend's face wondering why Brooke seemed to be bothered about having Jane over and decided to ask. "Brooke, why are you against Jane being here? What are you not telling me? Did anything happen between you two?" Lauren questioned.

Turning away from Lauren's prying eyes, Brooke said, "It's nothing. I'm just being childish. It will be good to see Jane again. But make sure you order from that Thai place we found a few months ago instead of pizza, it has the best food, and I'm starving," Brooke said with a smirk, but deep down, she dreaded the idea of seeing Jane. She couldn't help but wonder if Lauren was satisfied with her answer to let it all go, or would she bring up her reservations about Jane? Either way, Brooke was sure of one thing, tonight was going to be interesting.

Lauren laughed, "Sounds good, I'll call them and order, and Jane can pick it up on her way here. Now tell me all about London." As the two friends chatted, Lauren couldn't let go of the feeling something wasn't right between Jane and Brooke. She wasn't sure exactly what to do to try to fix it or if she should even get involved. Deciding not to press further, Lauren enjoyed catching up with the globetrotting Brooke while they waited for Jane and the food to arrive.

A short time later, Lauren announced, "Jane's here. Thank God, I am starving!"

"I've got food! Oh, hi Brooke, I didn't know you were in town. It's great to see you," Jane said politely. "How is London?"

Brooke wasn't sure how to be around Jane, let alone talk to her without wanting to yell. The anger that simmered at the mere sight of her set into motion a series of thoughts and feelings Brooke hadn't had to deal with since leaving San Fransisco. She didn't anticipate this encounter with her being so difficult. "London is fine," she said flatly, given it was the best Brooke could muster for enthusiasm.

Jane saw Brooke's face; her eyes were cold, without feeling, reminding her of the look in Damian's the night he left, sending chills down Jane's back. Did she hate her that much? And why? "I better take the food to the kitchen," she said, smiling slightly. As she walked past Brooke, she looked down to the floor. As she arranged the containers on the table and gathered plates and utensils, Jane wondered what was wrong given Brooke's attitude towards her. The last thing Jane wanted was to be a punching bag for something she had no idea was even a problem.

The silence between the two women was deafening, even with Lauren doing all of the talking about the wedding plans and work. She hoped the tension in the air would subside, but despite her best efforts, the two women remained quiet while passively listening. Lauren always felt Brooke didn't really like Jane for some reason, and tonight only seemed to confirm her suspicions.

Jane sat listening to Lauren while her mind questioned what was going on with Brooke. She sipped her wine, trying to formulate a good way to ease into a conversation, extending an olive branch to Brooke in the hopes of clearing the air, or perhaps, making things worse. Nonetheless, Jane knew she wasn't going to sit there any longer, feeling Brooke's cold disposition towards her. Jane decided to ask, "What brings you back to San Fransisco?"

Brooke had to admit she was a bit relieved that Jane made the first move to engage in conversation with her. Deep down, Brooke had many mixed emotions and wasn't sure how best to respond to her. Lash out and risk looking like a jealous child or be more of an adult? *Ugh*, Brooke thought to herself, *adulting sucks!* "A company has a large marketing project for their European and US offices, so I'm back for some meetings this week."

Jane smiled and said, "Great," then took the last sip of wine, unsure of what more to say. The truth was, she didn't completely understand what Brooke or Lauren did for work, specifically concerning marketing, so Jane often listened passively to any conversation they had regarding work.

"Jane, you need more wine. Come with me," Lauren summoned as she took Jane by the hand and led her to the kitchen, giving her a stern look as if to say there wasn't an option.

"Why are you looking at me like that?" Jane whispered as she poured a glass of wine for herself. Lauren didn't say anything; however, silently standing with her hands on her hips, she stared at Jane, clearly with something on her mind. "What?" Jane asked with some hesitation, unsure if she wanted to hear what her friend had to say or not.

"You know what," Lauren accused.

Jane looked at Lauren, dumbfounded and confused. "No, actually, I don't know what you are getting at."

Lauren sighed impatiently, "Why are you and Brooke acting like you can barely stand to be around one another?"

"I don't know what you are saying. I just asked Lauren what brought her back here," Jane said, not understanding what the problem was.

Unconvinced, Lauren asked, "So, nothing is going on between you and Brooke?"

"No. I've always felt like she wasn't my biggest fan. But other than that, no, I don't have any reason to not like Brooke, Jane replied.

Lauren looked at her, confused about Jane's comment about Brooke not liking her, but as she was about to ask Jane to clarify, Brooke poked her head around the corner, startling them both.

"Hey! It's taking some time to get that wine," Brooke commented.

"Just getting the leftovers from dinner put away," Lauren replied as she quickly turned away from Brooke to appear busy.

But Brooke wasn't fooled, as she heard the conversation between Lauren and Jane and decided it was time to get to clear the air. "You do realize I can hear you both? So, let me start."

Brooke took the wine bottle, poured the last of it into her glass, and took a sip. Thinking about what she was going to say, Brooke felt it was best to be straightforward. "I am troubled, Jane, because you and Gabriel became good friends, and neither one of you felt as though it was important enough to tell me. The more time you two spent together, the more his curiosity about you grew. It seemed like you were flattered having his interest while your relationship with Damian was on the rocks. If you weren't happy with him, you decided to snake your way into my relationship to make yourself feel better. She then took another sip of wine, unsure of what to do or say next. She chose to wait and see what the fallout of her outburst was to bring.

Neither Jane nor Lauren understood what had just happened. Lauren stood in shock, speechless for one of the few times in her life. She saw the colour drain from Jane's face, and her eyes well with tears as her hand began to shake, forcing Jane to set her wine glass down on the counter.

Jane didn't know what to do or what to say. Why would Brooke think these things of her? How could Brooke believe she had any interest in Gabriel? All of the conversations Gabriel had with her were about the issues with Damian, so Jane struggled to understand why Brooke felt the way she did. Unable to meet Brooke's stare, a tidal wave of guilt hit Jane as Brooke's words seeped into her consciousness. Maybe what Brooke said was true, making Jane doubt her intention towards him. Unknowingly, perhaps she did give the impression she was interested in him. She was the perpetually helpless, timid girl, seeking help and advice, mostly where Damian was concerned. It didn't occur to Jane how it might look to Brooke. Jane's heart sank as her tears tumbled down her cheeks. Unable or may be unwilling to look at Lauren or Brooke, Jane needed to be on her own and decided it was time for her to leave. Without saying a word, Jane got her purse, then walked to the front door, leaving it open slightly behind her.

Lauren raised her hands in the air and exclaimed to Brooke, "What the hell was that?! before she turned and ran after Jane. Brooke stayed in the kitchen, leaning against the counter, sipping her wine with a feeling of satisfaction.

Jane reached her car and was about to find her keys when she heard her name.

"Jane, please stop. Don't leave!" Lauren called out.

Jane spun around. "I'm not feeling very well. I would like to go home!"

"Jane, I'm sorry, but you can't leave. You and Brooke need to talk this out. Please!" she said with desperation in her voice.

She heard Lauren's words, but the idea of facing Brooke again only made her humiliation and guilt worse.

"Jane, you weren't responsible for their break up. You can't seriously let her get to you. They were going to end things when she got her promotion. It was inevitable." Lauren put her hands on Jane's shoulders. "Listen to me, Jane. You have to come back inside. Please don't go."

Jane heard her friend's plea. But anger quickly rose within her, dissipating the self-inflicted guilt. Why would Brooke blame her for their breakup? Why would Brooke keep all her feelings of resentment to herself if that was how she truly felt about her? Was Brooke just trying to be hurtful and inflict humiliation for some self-serving reason? It wasn't fair, and with that in mind, Jane decided not to let Brooke have the final word. She had nothing to be ashamed of. In fact, it was Brooke who should feel bad for how she chose to deal with her frustrations towards her. Rather than ambushing her in front of Lauren, they should have talked like adults instead. Jane wondered if Brooke planned on having Lauren's support. As she breathed out a deep sigh, Jane began walking back to Lauren's without saying another word to Lauren.

"Jane? What are you going to do?" Lauren questioned with concern as she saw the look on Jane's face. Growing worried, she hoped Jane would reconsider whatever was going through her mind. "This is not how I thought this evening was going to be," Lauren hesitantly added. Lauren wasn't sure what to do or say for one of the few times in her life.

Jane heard Lauren as she walked away and thought about how to resolve this challenging predicament without sacrificing or further damaging an already fragile friendship. She wasn't sure what to do about the situation other than to talk to Brooke about it, but one thing had become crystal clear to her, it wasn't her fault Gabriel and Brooke broke up, and she wasn't about to be the punching bag Brooke deemed her to be. She realized, too, that no amount of success made Brooke immune to the emotions of a broken heart, and it diluted the anger Jane felt as she paused at the base of the front steps.

Lauren saw Jane hesitate and felt a huge sigh of relief come over her. She decided to meet Jane where she stood. Hugging Jane, Lauren said, "Things will be ok and will sort themselves out. Please don't go. Talk to her, Jane."

Jane knew deep down Lauren was right, but she also knew her friendship with Brooke was forever changed. There would always remain a sense of apprehension and distrust between them, which left a distasteful bitterness in the pit of Jane's stomach. But despite everything, Jane knew she needed to confront Brooke, if for no other reason than to reclaim within herself some respect and strength. It was then or never as she walked through the front door, with Lauren in her shadow.

As Jane and Lauren walked into the living room, they found Brooke sitting sipping her wine while typing away on her cell phone, disregarding their presence. Her blatant disdain grated on Jane's nerves. How dare she accuse her of being the reason she dissolved her relationship with Gabriel in the manner she did. Jane wiped away any evidence of the tears shed earlier, mustering the courage to approach Brooke as a mature adult and with dignity. "Brooke, I would like to say I am sorry. Sorry for causing any distress between you and Gabriel. That was never my intention, and to be honest, I wasn't aware I was doing anything perceived as wrong. At no time did you or Gabriel come to me to communicate your concerns, which I feel would have helped me understand your feelings, rather than attacking me today. We are all adults, and I will not allow you to treat me with so little regard."

During Jane's speech, Brooke sat with her phone in hand but heard every word. It was clear to Brooke that Jane had gathered herself and decided it was time to deal with things and stand up for herself. Little did she understand, though, Brooke was not in the mood to talk to Jane but felt compelled to do so, given she had returned with the intention of doing just that. "You have a lot of nerve telling me I have little regard for you. You were someone I considered a friend," Brooke challenged back.

"I thought we were friends, but you and I both know that was a lie. I am not equal in your mind. I am just a nurse instead of a director in a successful corporation like you. That in no way makes me less than you in any way. You have never considered me a friend; if you had, you would have never treated me like you did tonight. Your breakup with Gabriel is between you and him. Do not put your remorse about your breakup with Gabriel on me. That is all yours, not mine to carry."

Without waiting for any rebuttal from Brooke, Jane turned around and gave Lauren a quick hug and said, "I'll call you tomorrow." She then picked up her jacket and purse and walked out the front door with her head held high, never looking behind her.

Left behind in Jane's wake was a fuming Brooke and an uncertain Lauren, who desperately needed a drink as she took her glass of wine and drank its entire contents before looking at Brooke. With the liquid courage on board, her stomach reminded Lauren she was still hungry, as she hadn't finished eating dinner yet when WWIII broke out. Brooke ate a spring roll with her fingers while she thought about what she would say to ease Lauren's frustration about this evening's blow-up.

"I'm sorry, Lauren. I don't know what came over me or why I reacted the way I did when I saw her. I felt an uncontrollable urge to lash out at Jane."

"No matter what happened between you and Gabriel, it wasn't Jane's fault. I don't understand why you would think it was," Lauren questioned.

Brooke felt unsure whether or not she was ready to confess to Lauren something she barely wanted to admit to herself. The very idea of even hearing herself say the words made her feel sick. "I don't hate Jane. In fact, I wish I was more like her. I am so used to being in control all the time at work, and in my personal life, it is exhausting. I would love to be more easygoing and less rigid in my expectations for myself and others because I am sure that is why I can't hold onto a relationship. I'm afraid. It feels like I have to choose between my career or love. Jane has had both, and I both admire and resent her for that." Brooke's admission of her frustrations and fears, locked away tight for so long, finally came out in the open, causing Brooke to feel exposed and emotional.

"Brooke, you will have both one day. Here and now might not be the right time. But don't believe love isn't going to happen for you," Lauren encouraged. Much to Lauren's surprise, Brooke's eyes misted over with tears. In all the time she had known her, Lauren had never seen such emotion from Brooke.

"You and Jane have had love and a career. What am I doing wrong? Why can't I have the same? I just don't understand!"

Lauren understood despite the put-together, professional exterior Brooke presented to the world, she was a woman who just wanted to be loved, seen, and heard. She was like every other woman. Lauren stood up and walked over to her defeated friend, wrapping her arms around Brooke's shoulders while she quietly wept.

A few minutes later, Brooke moved from Lauren's embrace and simply said, "Thank you," then walked to the bathroom.

In the meantime, Lauren texted Jane.

You need to come back. It wasn't about you at all. I know you two can talk things through. You'll see.

Jane read Lauren's text, and deep down, knew her friend was right. Perhaps that was why she hadn't driven away yet. Jane sat in her parked car, pondering whether to leave or go back inside and face Brooke's displeasure again. She couldn't help but wonder what made Brooke so upset. "I must be a glutton for punishment," Jane said out loud to herself while she got out and walked towards Lauren's condo. Taking a deep breath in, she paused a moment before knocking on the door. She sighed. "What am I doing here?" Jane whispered as she shook her head in dubiety. "I hope I don't regret this," she said as she knocked a couple of times, then opened the door slightly. "Hey, it's me."

Chapter 15

Jane quietly sat down, unsure of what to expect and second-guessing her decision to return. Was she hoping for an apology from Brooke, or perhaps she wanted to make an effort to resolve whatever issue Brooke had against her? Whatever the reason, it was essential to Jane that they not pick up where they left off and continue arguing. It was her hope they could let it all go and move forward. But everyone remained silent as if afraid, perhaps, of what would happen should Brooke and Jane start talking.

Lauren, who always seemed to know what to say, found the silence deafening and unbearable. Unable to take it any longer, she decided someone needed to say something. "For the love of God, could someone please apologize already?!" Lauren bellowed.

Brooke agreed. Someone did need to apologize, but she wasn't sure if she should be the one to do so, that was until Lauren gave her a side-eye look. Guess she was going to be the bigger person and start first. "I'm sorry, Jane. I shouldn't have attacked you like that. You are also not responsible for the way things turned out for Gabriel and me. I lashed out because I find it challenging to wrap my head around the two of you being friends. I just wasn't prepared for that news. I do feel a bit bad about not taking the news so well and taking my anger out on you tonight. I am sorry."

Jane felt Brooke's apology was slightly backhanded, but hearing she wasn't the reason for their demise gave Jane some relief. But Brooke's apology didn't remove fully the anguish left behind from their argument. It wasn't right; however, was it worth it to put Brooke in her place by starting another fight? Ultimately, Jane decided no, it wasn't and chose to take the high road and say, "I'm sorry too." Deep down, Jane didn't honestly believe she needed to apologize for defending herself to someone who had insecurity issues with her former boyfriend. Perhaps it was best to leave some things left unsaid, and this was one of those times.

Brooke wasn't used to apologizing for anything, and having to say those words to Jane made her sick to her stomach. It was painful to look at Jane and know Gabriel was intrigued by her. The truth was, Brooke never wanted to leave Gabriel but didn't feel there was a choice when the promotion was out of the London office. She had earned it with all of the late-night meetings and marketing project planning sessions over the years. Of all the eligible people Brooke worked with, she knew the promotion was hers. There was no way she was about to pass over an opportunity of a lifetime that could lead to her having her own marketing firm one day. Once she had gotten herself settled in London, Brooke knew she made the right decision. It wasn't until Lauren had told her about Gabriel and Jane being friends that she felt the sting of knowing what she had given up for her new job. Why couldn't she have both the job and the man? Why was there always an impossible choice to be made?

Brooke took a sip of wine as she recalled the conversation, which had her believe ending their relationship was for the best. What would people think about Gabriel if they knew the truth about him? He was a gorgeous, mysterious man to many admiring feminine hearts and a successful entrepreneur within the business community. But there was a secret about Gabriel that Brooke was sure she was the only woman he told until she wondered if Jane was also aware of his secret life. Should she say something to Jane? Would she even believe her, as it had initially seemed so far-fetched, even to Brooke, after he had told her? Would she be doing the right thing by telling the girls? If Gabriel and Jane were going to have a friendship, intimate or not, Brooke decided she should know. Perhaps then, things would run their course, and it would no longer be a thorn in her side and a dagger to her heart.

There was no time like the present, Brooke thought, and she said, "The reason why I struggled with the break up with Gabriel wasn't just about my promotion; there was another reason I haven't told anyone about." Both women remained silent despite their curiosity growing ever impatient. "Gabriel is into BDSM and kinky sex. He asked me to consider exploring it with him. He asked me to be his submissive. But I hadn't had the chance to tell him about my promotion, so after we talked, everything changed between us. With my professional life changing so fast, I wasn't sure how to handle the added stress of knowing my boyfriend wanted to tie me up and fuck me, and God knows what else. It was all so shocking and added to the stress of things. Jane, I know you were not to blame for our break up, but he has an affinity towards you, and I'm not fond of that. I should have talked to you about it before, but I didn't think of it as something that would bother me as much as it has. If you are to continue your friendship with Gabriel, I feel you have the right to know about this part of his life.

Both Jane and Lauren had a look of surprise on their faces as they processed what Brooke had just confided to them. Lauren looked at Jane, but neither one said anything, prompting Jane to turn her back to them so as not to give away any hint of her interest in a BDSM lifestyle. Was it the fascination of exploring new things with a man whom she found intoxicating? Or perhaps, there lived something inside her, which Jane wouldn't admit to, as a hunger to explore erotic fantasies, like the ones she and Damian did together. To Jane, Gabriel was unique and enchanting beyond any of her wildest imaginings, and learning about his BDSM desires only fueled Jane's curiosities further. What was she going to do now, knowing his secret?

"Jane, are you ok?" Lauren asked as she saw the faraway look in Jane's eyes.

"Yup, just thinking," Jane said as she turned back to face her friends, hoping they couldn't see what she was musing about. Just as Jane turned around, Brooke stood in front of her. "Oh no," Jane thought.

But to Jane's surprise, Brooke asked, "Friends?"

Jane looked at Brooke before standing up. "Yes, of course," she said, but silently, Jane determined she was not without caution.

The two friends hugged, giving Lauren a sense of relief that things seemed ok between them. "I'm so happy!" Lauren exclaimed as she joined in on the hug.

"Are there any spring rolls left? I'm starving?" Jane asked.

The three women enjoyed an evening of wedding talk and hearing about Brooke's London adventures, with lots of laughs. However, one topic remained unspeakable, that was until Lauren decided to jump right in and ask, while thoughts of kinky sex teased her curiosity. Taking a sip of her wine, Lauren expressively gestured with her hands an intro to the hush-hush topic they avoided, well, until that moment. "So, tell me, Brooke, what exactly is Gabriel into when it comes to sex?" she said.

Brooke knew subtly was not Lauren's forte, but she also knew the conversation would come up; it was inevitable with her dropping a bomb like that out of the blue. "I'm not exactly sure. He hoped I would consider being his submissive. What that means exactly, I am not sure. What he explained to me was his enjoyment of kinky sex. He was a Dominant or a Dom, I believed he called it, and he wanted me to be his submissive."

"What did you say when he asked you?" Lauren eagerly quizzed, with Jane's own curiosity piqued. She was just as hungry to hear what Gabriel had talked about with Brooke.

"I wasn't sure what a submissive and a Dom were, but I wasn't about to ask him till I looked it up online. But I wasn't prepared for what I found, and I knew immediately there was no way I could participate in anything like it."

"What things exactly did you see?" Lauren eagerly asked.

Brooke hesitated before saying, "There were many horrid things, involving whips and chains, and even a woman eating out of a dog food bowl on the floor while wearing a leash. I found all kinds of crazy things, which had me wondering if he would expect me to do all those ridiculous things or maybe even hurt me physically. It's not exactly my kind of fun. It all seemed to be a lot more than I was willing to do for a man I loved, even Gabriel. Whatever happened to the idea of being in love and having a great relationship without any games? The stress of being something I am not felt awkward and demeaning. Then add on my new promotion in a different country with limited time to learn what it meant to be a submissive and manage all of my new responsibilities. It was all just too much! Brooke turned away and stared out the living room window, taking a sip of wine as she contemplated what life with Gabriel would have been like if she had stayed in San Fransisco.

"I can't believe he's into that crazy kind of shit!" Lauren said in disbelief. "I just looked up submissive and saw a woman tied to some cross and whipped! It's fucking crazy! There is no way anyone in their right mind would think that was safe or sane, for that matter! I can't believe Gabriel is into all that!"

"I can't see it being all about whips and violence," Jane offered innocently. "There has to be more to it than that? It can't be all bad; otherwise, why would people be interested in BDSM?"

"Jane, you can't be serious?" Lauren exclaimed. "You're saying you would consider a relationship like that or be willing to give up any control of your body for the sake of a man getting off on beating you?!"

Jane went a bright shade of red, and she felt a sudden surge of heat come over her. "Yes, and no," she replied with her back to Lauren so she wouldn't see her embarrassment, making it easier to talk without seeing the prying eyes of Brooke and Lauren. Maybe she was afraid of what they might see or assume about her. Perhaps keeping her thoughts vaulted safely away was something she should have done, but it was too late for any kind of discernment.

Jane sat down, with Brooke and Lauren eagerly awaiting what she was about to tell them. She went into how everything she experienced with Damian enlightened her to see possibilities and be less fearful of trying something new. Despite the woes of their relationship, Damian pushed Jane to discover the meaning of boundaries, which enabled her to discover a new world of intimacy. Together they watched porn and began experimenting through a common interest for variety in their relationship, one of which was D/s, or Dom/sub. Damian's strong dominant nature and her softer submissive one naturally fit together, creating the uniqueness of a connection created with opposite energies. Jane learned masculine and feminine spirits didn't mean specifically man or woman; rather, it was a person's authentic state of being. Every person possesses both within them, with some people taking the dominant persona, while others the submissive. Then there are those who fluctuate between the two energies, depending upon their needs at that moment, who refer to themselves as Switches. D/s was more than just sex. It was an inherent part of a person's soul. Upon understanding this part of herself, Jane looked forward to knowing she was protected and loved. What she hadn't realized was it could create the illusion of love and trust, just like any other connection could. It all boiled down to one thing: every relationship was based upon open, honest communication. Communication allowed for trust to be earned and a bond to thrive and grow. All of these traits, Jane believed, she had with Damian; however, it was all an illusion made up in her head. Damian was not loving or trustworthy, and in the end, created fear within her, destroying the trust she thought they had together.

Brooke took a sudden keen interest in the conversation, especially in Jane's reaction and thoughts about D/s. When Jane blushed, Brooke wondered how much she knew about that kind of lifestyle and sexual activity and suddenly understood Jane wasn't as naïve as she assumed her to be. No wonder Gabriel was enamoured with her. Jane was submissive in every way, while she was dominant by nature. She embodied everything Brooke wasn't, and likely she would never have made Gabriel happy or satisfied. Brooke needed the routine of control in her life and relationships, which fundamentally would have driven Gabriel away. She concluded, being assertive and strong-willed always seemed to make dating challenging, as her past relationships had proven, including the one with Gabriel, as she recalled the afternoon they met while at a business luncheon. Over the course of their bond, he shared with her how he yearned for a lover, girlfriend, and submissive for his twisted pleasure. There was no way she would ever bow down to a man; she was either equal or nothing at all to them. So, when the time came to make the decision between taking the new job or Gabriel, Brooke chose her career, leaving the door wide open for Gabriel to find what he wanted: Jane.

"You seem to know a lot about BDSM," Brooke proposed to Jane, purposely putting her on the spot.

Jane undoubtedly knew she was being challenged and decided to address it with tactfulness, hopefully giving some insight without giving away many intimate details of the relationship she and Damian had shared together. With luck, it would satisfy Brooke's intrusiveness. Truthfully, it was none of anyone's business; she had nothing to prove or explain. Jane contemplated how best to answer Brooke's impertinent questions, given how emotional the evening had already been. "Damian and I experimented," Jane began to say, then took a sip of her wine, waiting for some reaction from Brooke and Lauren.

"Well, well, well, who knew you had such a wild side, Jane. You are surprising despite my knowing you for most of your life," Lauren teased with a Cheshire cat smile. "And here I thought I knew everything about you," she said with a smirk and a wink.

Jane smiled at the dear friend she'd had since they were eight years old. She was a loner in school and liked to read quietly on her own while the other kids ran about the playground. One day, Lauren saw Jane sitting alone under a tree reading, so she wandered over and introduced herself. As Jane recalled the first time they met, Lauren was always very outgoing and took great pride in her ability to talk to anyone. She possessed a natural talent for making people feel at ease. That feeling resonated with Jane, even at a very young age, and since then, she and Lauren remained best friends, and it was true, Lauren did know Jane down to the most minute detail. They shared everything: first crush; first kiss; their deepest, most secretive thoughts. But once they grew up and began living their own adult lives, their communication changed, became less open, less honest.

Jane and Damian experienced problems in their relationship, which Lauren would have relished given how much she hated Damian. With the likelihood of being told, "I told you so," Jane concluded, if she confided in her best friend, there would be more drama than what she wanted to deal with between Lauren and Damian, and it would raise concerns about her being abused. Instead, Jane told Lauren certain things within the boundary of her comfort level. The sense of shame about her life with Damian over the last year created a wall that allowed Jane to keep many things hidden from Lauren. This was something that Jane wished was different. She missed her best friend and their once limitless, no-boundary conversations. Jane's lonely life with Damian allowed her friendship with Lauren to suffer while cultivating her low self-worth and lack of self-love in almost every area of her life.

Jane hadn't expected the turn of events of this evening, and more so, the conversation about D/s or BDSM. The idea of being labelled as weird, scared Jane, and now her worst fear was coming to fruition. She wanted to display a confident woman in front of Lauren and Brooke, but as thoughts of self-doubt clouded her courage, Jane began to second guess herself with the decision to come clean and let the chips fall where they may, instead of hiding in the shadows of her former life with Damian. What was she going to do? What was she willing to divulge to them without damaging her reputation beyond repair?

"Jane?" Lauren said with a sly smile. She knew Jane was holding something back from her and had been for a long time. She didn't know why, though. They shared so much in the past, but when Damian came into Jane's life, the two friends grew distant, much to her disappointment. Was Jane's relationship with Damian and their intimate life the reason why? "Jane, talk to me."

Jane looked at Lauren and then at Brooke. Maybe it was time to tell the truth about a piece of her life, and she took another sip of wine in the hope of finding some of her faded courage. "Damian and I...." and her voice trailed off as second thoughts plagued Jane. But she knew there was no turning back now. "Damian and I had a D/s relationship." There. She said it. It was finally out in the open. *Oh, God!* Jane screamed within.

Brooke and Lauren were silent as they looked at one another, speechless. Lauren's expression changed quickly from intrigue to concern as she realized what that possibly meant and asked, "Did he ever hurt you?"

"He didn't beat me if that is what you really want to know. There would be some hair pulling, spanking, and him holding me down. The sex could be demanding."

"You are surprising." Lauren winked at Jane, unconvinced Jane was being truthful and was still hiding something.

Jane just sat there, unsure of what to say as regret washed over her. Exposing her past with Damian to Lauren and Brooke was, in a way, reclaiming a piece of herself. But was it really? Was it worth it? She took a sip of wine, thinking to herself how it didn't matter anymore. There was no taking it back now.

Meanwhile, Brooke sat quietly in thought. No wonder Gabriel was attracted to Jane. She literally would do anything for love, even if it meant doing some sexual acts to keep them happy and interested in her. Jane really was pathetic. How could she be so naïve and dumb! Despite her apology to Jane earlier, Brooke couldn't shake the jealous dislike she felt towards Jane or the idea of Gabriel's interest in Jane's submissive side. Who the hell did Jane think she was?!

The atmosphere suddenly shifted between Jane and Brooke. Jane couldn't dismiss the change in Brooke's body language, while Lauren seemed to overcompensate with sweetness towards her. Ugh! This entire evening couldn't be more of a disaster! She couldn't wait for it to be over, then she could retreat to her safe haven and forget all about this horrid evening.

Lauren couldn't help but ask for more information as she was now both concerned and intrigued by the type of relationship Jane and Damian shared. Perhaps that was their downfall, or partially anyway. "So does that mean it is all about kinky sex, or what exactly does it all involve?" Lauren pushed.

Jane wished she had never said anything and wasn't sure how many more questions she could answer. A heavy sigh escaped her chest at the thought of having to explain everything she was desperate to bury about her relationship with Damian. Their life together wasn't purely all about D/s. "Our sex life was where we experimented. You can make D/s whatever you want. Sexual only, or defining roles in other areas of a relationship or life. Who does the house cleaning, how to dress, who works, etc. It can be about many areas of life, not just about sex," Jane replied.

"So, it is between the two people to decide what D/s means to them and how they chose to live their life together? I find this all fascinating! said Lauren.

"Shocking!" Brooke said flatly, uninterested. The poisonous jealousy towards Jane grew harder and harder to conceal with every word that came out of her mouth. She had had enough. "Well, ladies, I'm going to head to bed. Jet lag is a bitch," Brooke abruptly announced. "Good night."

The immediate frigid demeanour of Brooke's disposition was too much for Jane to take, and she decided now was a good time to take their dishes to the kitchen in the hopes of escaping it.

Lauren showed Brooke her room and said good night. As she walked towards the kitchen, Lauren pondered what she would say to Jane. It became clear to her that she didn't really know Jane as well as she used to and wondered what part perhaps she played in that. Lauren saw Jane's look of defeat while she put the dishes in the dishwasher and felt the need to make amends with her longtime friend. Lauren came up behind Jane and wrapped her arms tightly around her. "I'm sorry it was a rough evening for you. And I'm so very sorry for not realizing how things were with Damian and not being there for you. I feel really terrible and wish I could change things."

Jane's eyes filled with tears as she hugged Lauren back. "It's not your fault. I didn't tell anyone."

Lauren smiled. "Please know you can come to me anytime about anything. I miss us! I'm not sure what changed or when, but let's promise we don't let things go unsaid going forward from tonight. Let's be honest no matter what, ok?"

Jane nodded. But deep down, she knew Lauren and Brooke would never understand about some of her sexual past, making it nearly impossible for her to be uninhibited about sharing details of her life with them. Brooke felt threatened by Jane, which seemed ludicrous to her, while Lauren was overly eager to be entertained by Jane's past. Neither situation was favourable, Jane concluded. As she walked to her car, she looked up at the star-filled night sky and wondered if there was any chance Brooke's notion of Gabriel being interest in her held any truth. Was Gabriel Lockhart really interested in her?

Chapter 16

Jane heard her text message notification sound and read the message from Lauren.

Hi. Sorry I haven't been in touch sooner. Hey, can I call you?

Jane replied,

Sure.

No sooner had Jane hit the send key when her phone rang.

"So, you really took me by surprise the other night, Jane. I felt bad about putting you on the spot like we did. Just wanted to say sorry."

Jane had been distant since that night, deciding to give some space between them. "No worries. I know I did. But you both pressured me to explain myself and go into details about my relationship with Damian."

Lauren hesitated for a moment before choosing to say, "I appreciate you being willing to talk to Brooke and me about things you and Damian experienced. Hearing Gabriel is into kinky sex and how you and Damian experimented in it as well was just a lot to take in. I was concerned Damian abused you, especially when I saw you with occasional bruising on your arms. And as it turned out, he was, at least in my opinion."

Jane sat on a bench in the hospital garden area, enjoying the late afternoon sunshine on her lunch break. A little quiet time to herself enabled Jane to think about the conversation with Lauren.

When the girls assumed her relationship with Damian was abusive, Jane succumbed to feelings of shame and worthlessness. Their intimate life was forceful at times, leaving behind some bruises, which she did her best to hide. In the last couple of years of their connection, Jane attempted to talk to Damian about the frustration he seemed to take out on her, but it only seemed to increase his annoyance, which made their intimate life more challenging. Jane found herself often making excuses for his behaviour, deflecting the blame upon her, knowing she did something which angered him. Despite the defiance which afflicted their relationship, Jane believed they could work things out. But it took their violent breakup and the loss of their baby to push Jane out of enabling mode and into finding her independence and strength. It wasn't an overnight process. It would take time. Moving into her own place was a start. What she hadn't anticipated, though, was parts of her life threatening the calm Jane was striving to find. As Lauren and Brooke questioned her about the kind of connection she had with Damian, Jane found herself wishing her friends would give her some credit rather than making her feel incompetent and small, incapable of managing her own life.

"Slacking off, I see," a male voice said jokingly behind Jane.

"Hey, Lauren, can I call you tonight, or I can stop by after work," she hurriedly said, grateful for the welcomed interruption. "Ok, love you too."

Putting her phone down, she turned around to find Justin standing behind her. "Ha, ha, ha," Jane mocked. "How's the shift going?

"It's going ok, nothing too exciting. I was making my last round of the grounds before the end of it. Saw you sitting here and came to say hi."

The two chatted a few more minutes before Justin suggested, "We should meet for a coffee one evening."

Jane looked at Justin and smiled. "Oh, I'm waiting to get my work schedule; maybe we can arrange something soon," she replied with some hesitation.

"Sounds great." He smiled. "I better get back to work. Chat with you later."

Why did life have to be so complicated? She recalled the evening with Lauren and Brooke, then, to add to her soul's dismay, Justin's interest in her. It was very troubling to Jane. She recognized she would eventually have to settle any assumed interest that Justin believed she had for him. The opportunity to be more than friends seemed to come about after her collapse at the hospital, making it almost feel like she owed him in some way. He was not her type and any suggestion in his head that she shared a mutual interest in being more than friends was simply untrue.

While Jane sat in the tranquil solitude outside, she reminisced about her limited yet educational experiences with men and saw some disturbing patterns, much to her dismay. She often failed to recognize or admit to herself that she was worth more than she received and was most often rendered as an object of convenience. Time and time again, Jane's heart gave much more than it received, and yet, the love and devotion she gave away never felt equally returned. Her needs often had a silent voice, leaving her to feel lonely, forgotten about, and used. It wasn't until she pondered the past that Jane saw how she enabled them. What was wrong with her?! How could she not see any of these issues before, especially with Damian?

In some ways, he was the worst one of all. Blinded by the love Jane had for him, she lost a part of herself, not discerning this till all was too late. Vying for his affection, Jane often felt needy and insecure, prohibiting a meaningful relationship to flourish in a healthy manner. Insecurity penetrated all facets of their relationship, driving Damian's desire to be with her farther and farther away. What she longed for most was to be loved, seen, and accepted for all she was, strengths and flaws alike.

But no matter how much Jane realized about herself in those moments, she knew she needed to make some changes; the only question was how? As Jane relished the sun's warmth on her skin, she lay down on the cushion of green grass, closing her eyes, and thought about how she would begin a journey of healing when she felt so broken inside. Her life was a far cry from what she envisioned as a college student it would be.

Jane still felt phantom abdominal pains every so often, which served as a constant reminder of the baby she once dreamed of having. It was difficult to believe her lonely existence, overwrought by her past with Damian, felt as though it would never release its grasp upon her. Would her life be this way forever? Would she be on her own, or would she share her life with someone who loved and adored her? Someone she could make memories with, raise a family together, and have the fabled happily ever after she desired most. Maybe it was too much to wish for. Perhaps being happy with the life she was living now was best. She had good friends, a great job, and a place to call her own. But even though she knew that was all true, Jane couldn't let go of the nagging what-if thoughts. Maybe she wouldn't have a love that was given to her equally. Then another text message hijacked her thoughts. It was Gabriel.

Hi, Jane. I was wondering if you might be free to meet me this evening for dinner?

Upon reading his message, Jane's body froze, and her pulse raced. Her phone slipped from her hand to the ground as she questioned what she was going to do. What was she going to say back without sounding like a babbling idiot? *Oh, God. Dinner! With her?!*

Hi. Wow, so surprised by your message, I dropped my phone.

How was she going to decline his invitation? As Jane waited for a reply, she thought to herself, would it be wrong if she did go for dinner with him? The truth was, she was fascinated with him: his pure masculinity mixed with his notoriously gorgeous dark looks that no doubt made almost every woman near him weak in the knees and blush like a young schoolgirl. They hadn't seen one another for a while but did send messages back and forth. So why now? Did he want something? She was single and available, as was he, so what was the big deal? Why couldn't they go for an innocent dinner?

Ding went her phone again.

LOL… did you find it?

Jane smirked to herself as she typed her reply.

Nope. I'll text you when I do.

Sassy! I like it! So, dinner tonight?

Jane texted,

I'm working till 7 p.m. Not sure if meeting around 8 p.m. would be too late or not for you?

Not at all. Let's have dinner at the brewery. We will have the place to ourselves at 9 p.m. when we close. I look forward to seeing you tonight.

Jane sat, trying to wrap her head around what had just happened. Did she just agree to meet Gabriel for dinner tonight?! "Oh God!" she said out loud. "This was not good! She had to cancel it. There was no way she should have accepted his invitation. What was she thinking?! Just then, the alarm on her phone rang, indicating her break was over. She now had to find a way to focus on work, knowing she was going on a date with Gabriel tonight.

The remainder of Jane's shift seemed to fly by in a blur when one of her co-workers said, "It's home time, girl. Got any plans tonight?"

Jane's face flushed, and she quickly lowered her gaze to the floor in fear of her co-worker seeing her cheeks redden. "Oh, not much. Probably hang out, watch TV, order some take-out. Nothing too exciting. How about you?"

"These tired old feet and I are going to bed," the woman said. "Well, my dear, have a good evening."

"Thank you. You too," Jane replied quietly back as the older woman walked out of the staff change room.

Jane walked out of the elevator into the vast hospital lobby and past the security desk, where she gave a small wave to Justin, who smiled and waved back. Jane knew she didn't want to date Justin. They weren't compatible. She also knew that they would have to talk one day soon, and she dreaded the very idea. Despite the dread Jane felt, she couldn't dwell on something that was in the future, and instead, the butterflies in her stomach reminded Jane she had a very exciting evening ahead.

Ding went her text message notification. It was Lauren.

Hey girl, whatcha doing? How was work?

Not much, just leaving work.

Jane wasn't going to tell Lauren about her dinner date with Gabriel, especially after the conversation they'd had the other night.

Instead, the two women chatted by text for a few minutes while Jane walked to her car. From a short distance away, Jane saw something on her windshield.

Jane texted, distracted from their conversation,

There is something on my car.

What?

There appeared to be a small bouquet of daisies wrapped prettily, tied with a satin ribbon.

There are flowers on my car.

Lauren sent an emoji pondering face.

Who are they from?

I don't know. Oh wait, there's a note.

Jane reached out for the small card. There were three words written in blue ink: *from an admirer.*

Lauren sent a surprised face emoji.

From an admirer? Do you recognize the handwriting?

No, I don't. I have no idea who put this on my car.

Jane paused, thinking about the possibilities. *I wonder.*

I might know who it is.

Lauren impatiently typed back.

Oh? Do tell.

I think it might be Justin. He talked to me today at work about going on a date one day soon.

What did you say back to him?

I said maybe. I didn't promise anything as I don't really want to go out with Justin.

Why wouldn't you? You haven't been on a date in a long time. You're going be a reclusive old maid if you don't get out, Jane. It might be a good thing.

Lauren's jab felt like a sharp knife plunged into Jane's chest.

Maybe.

She wasn't interested in Justin romantically. Just because she didn't want anything more than friendship with Justin didn't mean she would become a recluse. It was essential to her to have mutual feelings with someone, rather than forcing a relationship for the sake of pleasing others or to not feel alone. It would be authentic, or it wouldn't happen at all.

We will see, Lauren. I better go. Have some errands to do. Love ya.

Ok, chat later. Love you.

Jane got home and quickly hopped into the shower, preoccupied with what she needed to do to get ready for her dinner date with Gabriel. Wiping her hand over the steamed-covered mirror, Jane saw herself staring back. Several questions churned incessantly in her mind: would things be awkward between them? Was this a dinner as friends, or was there something more? Would tonight change everything in their friendship? All kinds of what-if scenarios ran through Jane's head while she got herself ready. Apprehension and doubt filled the eyes of the woman who stared back at her in the mirror. So many questions with no answers.

Jane whispered to herself while standing in front of the open closet. Casual or dressy? Pants or a skirt? "Argh!" Jane said out loud as the pile of clothing grew on her bed. Seeing herself in the full-length mirror wearing dark-blue skinny jeans, a white T-shirt, black ankle booties, and a grey leather jacket. Finishing off her overall look, Jane put in her favourite silver hoop earrings, a bracelet with a shiny star charm, and a white gold ring. "There. Well, that's as good as it is going to get," Jane said in a whisper. Shiny hair with soft waves, and pretty yet subtle makeup, with one final touch of a spritz of her favourite perfume, completed her overall look. Despite how she looked, Jane hoped it was enough, that she was enough. "Damn! I'm going to be late," Jane said as she quickly walked to the front door, grabbed her keys, and left, leaving the flowers she found on her car earlier on the entryway table. There wasn't any time to put them in water, or she would be late for sure.

They watched Jane leave from across the street, wondering where she was going in such a hurry. They couldn't help but notice how beautiful she looked as they took a drag from a cigarette. They waited to pull out a few cars down from Jane's as she drove down the street. "Someone's in a hurry," they said, realizing if they didn't speed up, Jane would be out of sight. "Where is she going?" they questioned out loud while headed towards the Golden Gate Bridge. But it wasn't in their favour to remain so close behind Jane, as the last light before the bridge turned red. "Ah fuck!" they growled, deciding last minute to run the light, forcing several oncoming drivers to come to an abrupt stop. Out of frustration, several honked at the reckless truck driver. *That was close,* they thought, but they couldn't risk losing Jane.

Jane finally arrived at the brewery to find the parking lot mostly empty, except for a few vehicles. Sitting in her car, not wanting to rush in just yet, Jane looked one last time in the mirror as she reapplied lip gloss. The same uncertain look stared back at her. Was he going to like spending time with her tonight? Or perhaps, he would find her boring and decide to end the evening early. It didn't really matter, as it was too late to cancel, and it would be incredibly rude to stand Gabriel up.

The walk towards the grand front doors was always stunning, Jane thought, as the pathway lights cast a soft glow across the shrubs and trees. But even the serene walk to the entrance couldn't distract Jane from the doubt which plagued her since receiving Gabriel's dinner invite. "Just breathe," Jane whispered to herself as she paused before walking inside the brewery.

Parking their truck on the road just at the brewery parking lot entrance, they saw Jane pause before entering the building. Who was Jane meeting here? Was it a date? The uneasiness of not knowing who Jane was meeting or what she was doing here aggravated them. They got out of the truck and leaned against the side, contemplating what to do next as they lit a cigarette. They didn't like not knowing the details of who she was meeting or why, but they had every intention of finding out for themselves. It didn't matter how long she would be. They would stay for as long as it took to find out what they needed to know. Thoughts about why Jane was at the brewery and who she was meeting there fueled their jealousy like gasoline on a fire. They would wait all night if need be. They looked out across the bay and tossed the butt of their cigarette to the ground before lighting another one. It would soon be dark, and then they would make their way towards the building under the cover of shadows. One way or another, they would find out who Jane was meeting.

Chapter 17

"Good evening Miss Riley. Let me show you to your table." A young woman smiled as she motioned for Jane to follow, leading her to a quiet table near the windows that gifted a patron a stunning view of the bay, the Golden Gate Bridge, and the city. The hostess said, "Mr. Lockhart will be with you in a few minutes. He sends his apologies."

Jane smiled and replied, "thank you," as she took a seat, marvelling at the scenic view and the rustic elegance surrounding her. The warmth from the stone fireplace and its soft glow created an intimate, cozy feeling, reminiscent of a cabin getaway, enjoying a roaring fire while curled up under a blanket. But as Jane looked around at the serene atmosphere, butterflies relentlessly fluttered inside her stomach while her heart beat a bit faster with anticipation that Gabriel would be with her soon. It was evident to Jane that he had put some thought into their date. It was all thought out, further making Jane feel both nervous and excited. Needing a distraction from the nervousness, Jane looked out to one of the most amazing views of the city. She got up and walked towards the large window, gazing out at what appeared to be millions of twinkle lights reflecting off the water as the sun began to set behind the hills, creating a beautiful water-coloured sky. It was truly breathtaking and perhaps one of Jane's favourite views of the cityscape.

"May I get you something to drink while you wait for Mr. Lockhart? He shouldn't be too much longer," a female voice asked, startling a distracted Jane.

"Sorry, I didn't mean to startle you," the young woman said. "Would you like something to drink while you wait?"

"It's ok. I should be paying more attention," Jane replied. "May I have a house red wine?"

The young woman nodded, vanishing as quickly as she appeared.

And just like that, the calming distraction Jane had moments ago dissipated like smoke into the air. The nerves reared their ugly head while her mind filled with insecurities about what to talk about. Perhaps he was late because he'd changed his mind. Maybe Gabriel realized the mistake he made and didn't know how to break the news to her. Too much overthinking cast unforgiving doubt within her heart. What was she doing here?

"I'm so sorry, Jane. My meeting went much longer than I wanted. I hope you weren't waiting long."

Jane jumped up from her chair, bumping the table. "Oh no!" Jane exclaimed as she tried to steady it back on its base. Embarrassed, she felt the heat in her cheeks as she lowered her head, taking in a deep breath in the hopes of casting away the clumsy little girl feeling. Jane turned around to face Gabriel. Upon first glance, Gabriel's piercing dark eyes bore right through to her soul, making it difficult to breathe as her heart raced faster than ever before.

Gabriel leaned against the stone fireplace with his arms crossed and a smirk on his face, trying his best not to embarrass the beautiful woman further. She had a way of making him smile, and he enjoyed that. "Everything ok?" he asked with a teasing smile on his face.

"Ah, yeah. You just startled me, that's all. Sorry," Jane replied, unsure of everything happening that very moment. Silently, Jane demanded of herself, *Get it together, Jane!*

Gabriel walked over to Jane, giving her a friendly hug in the hopes of easing her anxiety and making her relax. Gabriel was very much aware of the effect he had upon Jane, and one day, he hoped it would subside or disappear altogether.

"Thank you for coming tonight. I have really been looking forward to spending some time with you."

Jane felt tongue-tied and somewhat lost in knowing what to do when he drew her close to him. Fearing he would see how much she liked him, Jane withdrew from their embrace and instantly regretted it. Wishing she would have stayed in his arms longer, Jane feared she would reveal her true feelings for him, and that was something she wasn't prepared to do this night. *Ugh, how was she going to get through this dinner? Why did he want to meet her?* His heady masculine scent put a spell on her, imprinting upon her. She couldn't recall anything more inviting or intoxicating.

"Shall we?" Gabriel gestured, pulling a chair out for her.

Jane smiled shyly and said, "thank you," still reeling from being in his arms.

"My pleasure," he replied quietly and let his hand brush against her lower back ever so slightly. His touch was electric, sending sensual shivers across her back.

Gabriel couldn't help but notice how pretty Jane looked, with her hair cascading over her shoulders in soft waves and how her eyes seemed bluer than usual. Wondering what it would be like to run his fingers through her silky hair as his lips hovered just above hers played in his mind. Lately, it had become harder not to think about Jane as his ever-growing fascination for her deepened. Jane had no idea how much it meant to him seeing her sitting across from him. She was both beautiful and intriguing to him in so many ways, and he recalled how Jane's arms felt when they hugged him and how her hands rested upon his back. Her embrace was warm and gentle, despite sensing her reluctance to stay in his arms. The uncertainty within herself was apparent and made

Gabriel want, more than ever, to help Jane feel comfortable and protected around him.

As their friendship grew over the past several months, Gabriel came to see Jane for who she indeed was: kind, honest, resilient, warm-hearted, sassy, and compassionate. Despite all of the hardships she has endured, he continuously marvelled at the courage and strength she showed, even in her most troublesome moments. One such time he would never forget was seeing her pale, frail body lying in the hospital bed, still and quiet. It had Gabriel reconsidering his reservations in expressing how much she had begun to mean to him. He aspired to have Jane know how he felt, how he wanted to see her, to get to know her, and not just as her friend.

After Brooke left for England, Gabriel tried focusing on his interests and personal needs. From time to time, he visited the BDSM club, where he was once an active member, but he found his heart wasn't into it without someone special to share it with. Seeing the connections that the other Doms he knew had with their subs by their side had him yearning to protect, love, and cherish a submissive of his own. For him, the D/s connection was unlike most relationships he had experienced before in his vanilla life. Vanilla, seen as boring and routine, is often how the BDSM world views "normal" relationships. In truth, any relationship can feel ordinary, boring, and routine. When a couple's communication stalls, it undoubtedly affects their intimate bond, often resulting in a dire ending. Finding a special woman with whom he could explore an intimate D/s bond while enjoying all that a normal relationship offers were what he most ardently hoped for. He wished to share a bond with someone and form a couple that could confide their hopes, aspirations, and fears with open and honest communication and unconditional acceptance. He wanted to give someone his love, and in return, be loved.

As he thought about his relationship with Brooke, he concluded she was unable, or maybe unwilling, to understand his desire and need to exercise his dominance. She being someone who exerted control every day, hid her vulnerability away out of fear others would perceive her as weak or incompetent, rendering her a slave to the authority and discipline she had grown used to. Two dominant people in a relationship such as theirs made them too close on the spectrum of control. They would have eventually fought for control, causing them to resent one another rather than create acceptance.

Then there was Jane, who was not only special in his eyes, but innately submissive. Gabriel felt it deep within his soul, Jane was a submissive in every way, and it taunted him day and night. He wanted her to know he thought she was stunning and wonderful and hoped Jane might feel something similar for him. Gabriel believed she did, as evidenced by the way she cast her eyes to the floor in his presence or those moments when she blushed a pretty shade of pink when she was near him. Tonight, he wanted her to feel special, with the hope of talking about the possibility of continuing to see one another. For the first time in a long time, Gabriel was excited to see a woman he believed was his "one."

For a few hours, the couple talked over wine and dinner, discussing many everyday things and laughing a lot. Gabriel had asked about her becoming a nurse, her hobbies, and many other things. The more he listened, it was obvious to him that she enchanted him. While listening to her talk about her childhood, he gained a larger understanding of her and why she was kind yet fearful. Jane's past cultivated a fear of being abandoned, forgotten, and devalued, and until that moment, he hadn't understood. All of her past relationships ended with someone leaving her, choosing another over her, or unexpectedly being taken away. Gabriel listened intently as Jane shared the passing of her parents at the age of six years old. Returning to San Fransisco, her parents'car was hit by a transport truck just outside of Los Angeles, killing both of them. Jane's mom had no family as she was adopted, and both of her parents had passed years before, while her dad's mom was the only living relative Jane had at the time of the accident. Raised by her grandmother, Jane grew up loved, but it never replaced the loss of the love she had for her parents. Gabriel watched Jane recount the tragic loss, and his heart immediately went out to her. He was becoming aware of how her life had been affected by all of the hardships. Gabriel wanted so very much to wrap her in his arms and shield her from all of the hurt. More than ever, he realized. He sat in awe of her strength and resiliency.

Taking a sip of wine, Jane felt as though she had been doing all the talking, prompting her to ask Gabriel about his childhood. As he talked, her eyes focused upon his lips, captivated by their fullness, Jane wondered what his kisses felt like. Were they soft and supple, or firm and demanding? Was he a great kisser who would make her dizzy with desire, making her hunger for more? How she wished, she thought while looking into his gorgeous eyes without being fearful or insecure, which so often hijacked her confidence every time she tried. Listening to him speak, she noted the sound of his voice: deep, sexy, and calming. She fixated upon his mouth as though she were in a trance. He spoke with such confidence but without arrogance. *Kind as he is sweet and genuine, Gabriel is positively the most handsome man.* Jane had an affinity for tall, strong men and felt safe when by their side. While making love, their sensual yet masculine energy made her crave to feel their body on top of and inside her. But one of her favourite things was being wrapped up in a man's arms, feeling his chiselled chest against her cheek as she nestled into the crook of his arm. It was truly Jane's favourite place to snuggle into, describing the feeling simply as home. To Jane, being in her favourite place made it easy to close off the rest of the world, forget about her troubles and worries, and simply let go, even if only for a little while. Feeling the soft caresses of a lover's fingertips upon her bare skin lulled Jane into dreams with ease while breathing in their essence with every bewitching breath. God, how she missed being with a man!

"Would you like something more to drink?" Gabriel asked her, pulling Jane out of her erotic dream-like fog.

She shifted in her seat as the throbbing need between her legs left her salaciously wanton for him, something she hadn't felt before. What was happening to her? She had to get herself together and under control. Otherwise, she feared she would do something stupid and embarrass herself beyond any repair. Silently, Jane prayed to let her get through this night without it being a complete disaster she would never live down.

"Did you have enough to eat?" Gabriel asked as he poured the remaining amount of red wine into both of their glasses.

"Yes. I couldn't possibly eat another bite. It was delicious, thank you."

"You're welcome." Gabriel smiled. He was having a great time and pondered when would be a good time to talk to her about his heart's desire. Maybe this night wasn't the right time, and if that were the case, when would it be? For one of the few times Gabriel could recall in his life, he wasn't sure what to do, as he second-guessed himself.

The couple sat quietly for a moment, enjoying the view of the bay as the rippling water reflected the moonlight. It was a lovely evening and a perfect first date. Jane felt chilled and trembled as goosebumps pebbled her skin. As Jane reached for her leather jacket, Gabriel stood up, offering his hand to her. Without saying a word, Jane smiled and took it. Instantly, she revelled in the feeling of his fingers enclosing around hers. To her, it felt incredible and safe. He led her towards the fireplace, motioning for her to take a seat.

"Thank you, that feels nice." Jane quietly said, stretching out her arms, feeling the heat radiating from the fire.

Gabriel smiled, pausing a brief moment as he contemplated how to make their date last longer. He wasn't ready for their date to end, not yet. "Would you like a nightcap or something else to drink?"

Jane nodded, "Something warm would be lovely, thank you." After Gabriel left, Jane stood by the fire, luxuriating in the flames' warmth while watching their hypnotic dance. Jane felt all her fears and doubts about her time with Gabriel relax and dissipate. It was a wonderful first date, and she longed for it not to end, not yet.

Gabriel returned to see Jane enjoying the warmth from the fireplace, and he smiled to himself while admiring how the soft light captured the subtle honey highlights in her hair. She looked at ease for the first time in a long time; there was nothing more beautiful to him. A sense of pride washed over him as he watched her, recalling how much she had endured over the last several months. Yet, as she stood before him, unaware of his admiring gaze, she looked radiant and endearing. Jane captivated him in every way, enchanting his heart and soul. He wished for nothing more than to take Jane into his arms, hold her tight, and keep her protected from any more hurt and disappointment.

Gabriel couldn't help noticing the restaurant was finally empty, and the lights were turned down low, with only the shadows from the firelight to keep them company while the warmness blanketed them. It was their very own private sanctuary, perfect in every way. He set down the cups of hot chocolate on the table then said, "I hope you are warming up. I brought you something warm to drink."

Jane smiled, appreciating his kindness. "I am." She picked up a hot mug of chocolatey deliciousness, with its delectable aroma and a hint of Irish cream being a taste of pure heaven. She closed her eyes, savouring the chocolate, serendipitous moment beside a wonderful fire, in the company of an amazing man. This night was perfect in every way.

Gabriel walked towards Jane, taking in the ravishing view of the woman he was quickly falling for. To his delight, she didn't move from his advance. Jane stood in place, feeling nothing but calm. She didn't want to move, despite her usual routine of running away out of fear and self-doubt. Tonight she didn't want to run; she wanted to stay for once in her life and take a chance.

Gabriel stopped in front of Jane, taking one of her hands in his, and slowly caressing it. How soft and warm it felt in his hand. As Jane watched Gabriel stroke her hand, she felt her face blush, wishing it was the heat from the fireplace, as the atmosphere suddenly felt like it was 100 degrees. Unsure of what to do or how to react to his gesture, Jane cast her eyes to the floor until she could think of something to say instead of being tongue-tied with her mind blank. Gabriel knew she was unaware of the effect of her submissiveness tugging at his Dom ego. There was nothing quite so beautiful as seeing a sub yearn to please, to serve. The very sight of a sub with cast-down eyes glamoured a Dom, creating a thirst to control her desires and orgasms, a desire for her to present her wanton, lust-filled body in his trust. A trust built upon open and honest communication, protection of her well-being. All these things a Dom takes pride in: cherishing her, seducing her body with hedonistic expertise and charm, bringing out the purest essence of her submissive soul, rendering her exhausted, with panting breaths and beads of sweat trickling down her bare skin. Gabriel thought about how the power exchange between a Dom and sub creates a synergy of opposites, built upon a connection of earned, unquestioned trust. As the Dom within him surfaced more frequently over the last several months, Gabriel knew with all his heart he had found a woman, a sub, he desired very much. He had found her, his "ne" in Jane.

Month after month, Gabriel couldn't deny their connection, which grew over time, leaving him to question if he should pursue things further with Jane. How would he encourage their friendship to grow into something more? This question plagued him at night for weeks. Did he only imagine there existed mutual feelings of interest between them, given how Jane behaved around him? Earning Jane's acceptance and trust would take time, he undoubtedly knew, and no matter the length of time, he would be patient. He longed to be her lover and protector more than anything, but was it possible she believed it to be a foregone conclusion that he was a sexual predator? Yes, he had sexual needs, which were not of the vanilla or socially acceptable variety, but it was not something he needed all the time. BDSM was often predetermined by the uninformed to be deviant and abusive. With time, Gabriel would help Jane see and understand the basis of a healthy relationship: safe, sane, connected and more communicative than she had previously experienced with Damian. Having a woman in his life with whom he could be open and honest about his needs, wants, and dreams were a long-sought-after hope with many disappointments, casting his hopes into dormancy, that was until he met Jane.

With every stroke of his thumb upon the back of her hand, Gabriel saw her breaths become shallower while his own heart raced. The incredible woman who stood before him, shrouded in feelings of doubt and unworthiness, made him smile, stirring his masculine need with ease. She was a gift to be treasured, never to be seen as anything less. Gently, he guided her to step closer, nestling their hands into his chest, cradling her back. It pleased him immensely that she didn't resist his advances and instead seemed to welcome them. Jane followed Gabriel's lead as they began to dance in front of the fireplace. The radiant glow created an ambiance of passion even Jane couldn't ignore, thinking it had been years since she had experienced anything remotely this romantic. Letting down some of her defences defined by her past, Jane allowed herself to caress Gabriel's back. Every contour of his muscular definition beckoned Jane to continue. Feeling the strength beneath her fingers heightened her desire for more. Gabriel adored her affection, evidenced by how his muscles tensed then relaxed under her most tender touch. Intrigued by the effect she had upon him, her desire ached for more. Jane edged closer into Gabriel's body, but it was her mind and heart that played a tug-of-war game, each with their agenda. Her mind begged to stop and question what she was doing, while her heart pleaded to let go of any preconceived notions and just let go. Confused about her intentions, Jane rested her hand upon his shoulder where it was safe, with her mind claiming victory over her heart.

Gabriel was in heaven under Jane's tender touch, hoping she would ease into his arms and gracefully allow him to show her heart what she meant to him. He savoured their mutual desire for one another reserved previously within the confines of friendship, that was until this moment. Gabriel didn't want to hold back his feelings any longer. It was almost too good to be true to him that Jane allowed herself to feel his affection, feel his body, and hopefully, his heart. There was no more holding back; it was time. Jane followed his lead and stopped, thinking Gabriel had enough dancing. She broke their embrace, taking a step away, just as Gabriel caught her hand and held it firmly in his.

"Please stay," he said quietly, pulling Jane closer to him. "I have wanted to tell you something for a while, Jane, and I wasn't sure when the perfect time was. But I know that time is now. Gabriel gazed deeply into Jane's eyes and said, "You have ignited something in my heart that I haven't felt in a very long time. You beguile and charm me, Jane, unlike anyone has before."

For one of the few times ever, Jane held Gabriel's gaze, hearing every word he said while in the comfort of his arms. Her heart believed everything he said, but her head stood in the way, raising the question, why her? How was it possible he was interested in her? How? Gabriel's words repeated like echoes in a cavern as uneasiness seduced her mind, filling it with fear and misgivings about Gabriel's true feelings. Jane premeditated freeing herself from his desirous embrace as the madness of her worries consumed her every thought in those moments. But she wanted, no, she needed to share with Gabriel her heart's most ardent affection for him. Her mind fought back stubbornly, reaffirming the fearful objections of the failures of her past. *Why her?! Why now?!*

Seeing the fear cloud over Jane's pretty face, he was desperate to put to rest the doubts he knew mulled over in her mind. Recognizing the challenge of being overwhelmed with self-doubt and feelings of inferior self-worth, Gabriel thought it was best to show she was enough, more than enough. Convincing her heart, diminishing her mind's control, Gabriel gently lifted her chin, beckoning her eyes to meet his gaze. "You need to hear me, Jane. You are amazing; the very thought of you makes me smile. Since you came into my life, you have helped me realize what I need, want, and desire most of all. Jane, I want to be a part of your life, not as your friend, but as your lover. I want you."

Did she hear him right? Did she? Disbelief afflicted her mind, but every worry, every doubt was quickly cast away when Gabriel lowered his lips just enough to hover above hers. Her initial reaction surprised even herself. She stayed without trying to disentangle herself from Gabriel's embrace. Her every breath ceased to exist as anticipation of what was about to happen filled her body with trepidation. *Was this actually happening?* Searching his eyes for an answer, Jane found it in a tenderly placed kiss upon her lips. Gabriel lifted his head to see Jane's eyes still closed, with her lips still slightly parted. The temptation was too much for him to ignore, and before Jane could open her eyes, she felt Gabriel's lips part hers, teasing and enticing for more.

Jane's mind went blank, and her heart sprinted faster than she thought possible. Her inner vixen took over, devouring Gabriel's lips with her own as she cradled his face in her hands. Their kiss was heady with untamed passion. The fear Jane once believed would take away her every happiness ceased to exist at that moment, allowing herself to let go, thirsting and craving a man whom she believed was perfect. Jane moved her body into Gabriel's, and she thought she just couldn't get close enough, as her soft lips lusted for him.

A few moments later, reluctantly, Jane pulled away from their passionately intense kiss, only to see Gabriel's dark, mysterious eyes gazing lustfully at her. Her body was ravaged with a fury of excitement. She needed to take a moment to catch her breath before taking the leap and telling him how she felt. Jane needed to say the words, to hear herself tell the man she had been fascinated with, how much she desired him. "I want you too," she whispered against his cheek, feeling a rush of emotion surface, to her dismay, as a single tear trickled down to her cheek.

Gabriel felt the emotion of her passionate heart, a most precious gift of a woman who had captured his heart in every way. Leaning in, Gabriel gently kissed her tear away, tasting the saltiness upon his tongue, seeing her brilliant blue eyes glistening with more. Every tear that subsequently fell, he kissed away, one after another.

For the first time in her life, Jane didn't feel like a burden. Whenever she had cried around Damian, he told her to get it together in a cold, unfeeling way. Gabriel seemed to appreciate her expression of her feelings rather than regarding them as a hindrance. *This was really happening!* Gabriel wanted her as much as she desired him, and she couldn't be happier.

Leaning back from their embrace, Gabriel saw nothing but joy on Jane's pretty face. Cradling it in his hands, he gave her a quick kiss before walking to the bar. Jane took advantage of sitting down before her legs gave out, and she looked out the window into the blackness of night, illuminated by the cityscape of lights.

For so long, Jane believed Damian was her soulmate, her everything, until he wasn't. Despite their failed relationship, she finally understood that things happened for a reason, no matter how cruel the lesson was. Perhaps she wouldn't have ever met Gabriel if Lauren wasn't getting married and had her engagement party/dinner at the brewery. That night rushed back to her from its vault, as Jane recalled when Damian had abandoned her. While crying out in the garden, Jane remembered Gabriel's kindly spoken words of support, offering to arrange a ride home for her. Maybe it was fate or perhaps a coincidence they found one another. Whatever it was, the universe, fate, or luck, Jane was forever grateful.

"Here. We have much to celebrate," Gabriel said as he placed a glass of sparkling wine on the table for her. "Thank you for having dinner with me tonight, Jane. You have no idea how happy I am," Gabriel said with a smile.

Smiling at Gabriel, she saw the euphoria in his dark eyes and wondered how this was all happening? He was so different from the men in her past relationships, making Jane question why her? She knew comparing Damian to Gabriel was a futile venture, as they couldn't be more different in every way, causing Jane to wonder why Gabriel's interest in her was so profound for him. She couldn't help but feel like a character kissed by her knight in shining armour in a fabled fairytale. Jane silently scolded herself for believing in a happily ever after ending, as cliché and unrealistic as it sounded, but it was what Jane had hoped was possible with Damian. Falling out of love with her and looking for someone to fill the vacancy in his heart, Damian needed to leave Jane. With the time that had passed, she learned how much they were not right for one another. She had finally believed deep within that despite how tragic of an ending they experienced, it was for the best. Without all of the lessons learned while she healed from the loss of Damian and his baby, Jane would have remained in limbo, lost, and broken. Although Jane still felt unsure of herself, and at times she was still healing, she believed with all her heart that Gabriel was meant to be a part of her life. He was her guiding star, helping her to find her true north. They seemed drawn to one another like magnets, confirming to Jane there was indeed something special between them, even if she didn't understand it fully or even knew why. Maybe it was fate. Jane smiled to herself, and at that moment, decided to not question it but rather, to accept the precious gift of Gabriel's heart.

Chapter 18

From outside in the dark shadows, they watched the couple smiling, laughing, and enjoying dinner with wine. And then they witnessed the kiss. "What a fucking whore!" they whispered loudly to themself viciously. "Argh!" they growled as they paced back and forth under cover of the trees. Jealously grew with every passing minute of seeing them laugh and watching Jane's come-hither smiles. Hastily they tried pulling out another cigarette from the package, but it was empty, further fueling their anger and frustration. Everything was going wrong, and they felt out of control, throwing the crumpled cigarette package. "Argh! Dumb bitch. Should have known she was a slut!" Their anger rose rapidly with each flashback of the two embracing and their flirtations. Did she honestly believe she would be happier with that guy? Their resentment festered the more they thought about the two of them being together. "Fuck! "Fuck her!" Scouring the ground, they looked for something, anything. Finding a rock, they tossed it into the air, catching it over and over as they watched the nauseatingly happy couple from the parking lot while pacing like a bored stable horse. They felt their jealousy rising within them, never so intensely before. "Argh!" they yelled, throwing the rock to the ground.

Gabriel returned with two glasses of the delectable effervescent wine while Jane wondered if it was possible to be happier. A content sigh escaped her lips as she sat on the window sill, curious about what was going on in Gabriel's head about their time together as she casually watched him.

"See anything you like?" Gabriel teased as he caught Jane watching him and handed her a glass.

Turning a bright shade of pink, Jane stood up quickly, causing herself to be light-headed, and she tried desperately to recover from both the humiliation and near-fainting spell by steadying herself with one hand on the window. In moments such as this, Jane wished she had a witty comment to overcome the awkwardness she often felt, but as usual, she drew a blank. Stalling, Jane took a sip of the sparkling wine and said, "Thank you for everything tonight. It's been such a wonderful evening."

"Perfect. I'm happy you have enjoyed yourself; I know I have." Gabriel smiled, capturing her gaze with his.

With the brewery empty, all was quiet. It was as though the rest of the world disappeared, creating the perfect environment for them to be alone together. No amount of wit would take the place of what Jane most ardently wanted to show Gabriel. It was now or never; setting her glass down on the table, she paused for a brief moment before walking to where Gabriel stood leaning against a table, staring at her intently.

"Why, Miss Riley, what, may I ask, are you planning to do?" Gabriel teased in a husky, deep voice as she placed her hands on either side of his face.

"You'll see," Jane replied in a whisper and sly smile.

"Oh really? I can hardly wait," he whispered back while he slipped his arms around her waist.

An insatiable appetite for his kisses coursed through Jane as the need to taste him again left her wanton. Beneath her gentle touch, Gabriel's smooth, clean-shaven skin felt like velvet, reminding her of the softness of his lips as they beckoned to her. Jane dared to allow herself to be vulnerable with him, wanting so much to be the seductive, confident, sexual playmate most men often fantasize their mate to be. Jane secretly wished to be a hellcat kind of lover, but she couldn't ignore the fact that she was plain Jane, a less appealing version of her fantasy. Her desire to be touched, cherished and protected by a man she shared a passionate love connection with, where she could be herself without the fear of being rejected, felt like a hopeless wish until she met Gabriel. He always made her feel safe and accepted fully for who she was, never making her feel inferior or less than in any way. Jane knew it was she who looked for imperfections, often finding them, including hiding away her true feelings for Gabriel. As she locked eyes with him, all the emotions surfaced from the vault they were kept in for so long, desperately needing to be set free for the man who she lusted for, for the better part of a year.

Gabriel couldn't help but feel the curvaceousness of Jane's breasts against his chest as she leaned into him, standing on her tiptoes. It was impossible for him to resist her advances any further. He was engulfing Jane in his arms, looking deeply into her eyes, and she was charming him, much to his delight, as he stared intently into their blue abysses, rendering him weak to temptation. He devoured Jane's mouth.

Their enthusiasm was like kindling on fire just before it fully ignites. There was no denying their magnetism; it was impossible not to see and, even more so, not act on it. He was dominant, and she was feminine, a perfectly orchestrated pairing in the world of D/s. As passion compelled him, Gabriel picked Jane up and sat her down on the table behind them.

Instinctively, Jane wrapped her legs around his hips, pulling him closer to her. His hands sensually explored her back as his lips nuzzled her neck, sending cascading waves of excitement throughout Jane's body like fireworks on the 4th of July. Soft murmurs escaped her lips as she relished his touch and savoured the feel of his lips upon her skin; it was addicting! Was this moment really happening? The man whom Jane had privately thirsted for over the last several months was in her arms, and it was the safest, most wondrous place to be. She never wanted to leave.

Lost within the rapture of their passion, Gabriel and Jane were rendered oblivious to the shadowy figure moving closer to the windows to get an unobstructed view of the couple. At the mere sight of the passionate couple kissing with so much heat between them, they couldn't take any more torture. Their rage knew no boundaries, vexing them to take desperate measures to make them stop the insanity. Thinking about the rock they toyed with earlier, they quickly looked around on the ground for another. Finding what they were looking for, they took one last look at the two of them, completely enthralled with one another. Winding up, they threw the rock at the large window, then yelled, "Whore!" They quickly turned and ran towards the parking lot to the awaiting parked truck.

The rock sounded like a bullet, shattering the glass window into a million razor-like shards. Instinctively, Gabriel pulled Jane down to the floor, shielding her with his body until he thought there was no longer a threat to them both. Spinning Jane around to face him, brushing fragments of glass from her hair and clothing, Gabriel anxiously asked, "Are you ok?"

The concern was evident upon his handsome face and in his eyes as Jane looked at him. Her head spun as she frantically tried to comprehend what had just happened. But she could not speak from the shock and confusion that overwhelmed her. *What did happen? Did someone fire a gun at them? Why?*

Gabriel saw Jane's disorientation and bewilderment and took her by the shoulders; he surveyed her body quickly for any physical harm. "Thank God," he whispered out loud when he didn't find anything. But Gabriel couldn't dismiss the look of fear in her eyes as her body began to tremble in his hands. "You are ok. I'll protect you. You're safe with me, Jane," he said, holding her hands tightly in his. "I'll be right back. Stay down till I get back!" Gabriel said, placing his hands on her shoulders, ensuring Jane knew he would be back.

Running towards the front door, Gabriel called out to the nearest staff person, "Call the police, now!" He ran to the parking lot road entrance to see a person getting into a truck parked on the side of the road. Gabriel sprinted towards the truck, but he couldn't catch up as it quickly sped off, throwing a bunch of gravel behind it until the tires met the pavement. It was too dark to see the truck's colour, the driver, or the license plate, but it did have the passenger tail light out.

"Argh! No!" Gabriel yelled in anguish and defeat as he bent over, putting his hands on his knees, trying to catch his breath, watching the truck's tail light dim in the distance. Maybe his surveillance cameras caught something as to who did this, Gabriel thought to himself. He had to get the video downloaded for the police, who would be there soon, and he heard the wail of sirens in the not-too-far distance. There wasn't anything more he could do other than ensure Jane was ok.

Anger exploded deep as they slammed their hand against the steering wheel, growling, "Bitch! You will pay! This is only the beginning; you have no idea what I'm capable of." With that last thought, they hit the gas, making the tires squeal before gaining traction, blistering the pavement with tread marks. In the rearview mirror, a darkened figure appeared, running in a feeble attempt to catch up to the truck as they sped away. "Fucker, you took her from me!"

"Jane? Jane?" Gabriel called out as he ran through the front door.

"I'm ok, just shaken. Did you see who it was?" she asked, wrapping her arms around herself.

"No. I saw someone run to a truck, and that was all. I couldn't see the colour, plate, or the driver. Gabriel wrapped his arms around Jane's shoulders, kissing her cheek, "I'm just relieved you are ok. You aren't cut anywhere?"

"No, I don't think so," Jane replied as she looked down at her hands for blood. "Why would someone do this? I thought a gun went off. I was so scared you were hurt."

"I wouldn't let anything happen to you, Jane. I hope you know that," Gabriel said, stroking her cheek. He took her in his arms until he felt Jane's body relax in his embrace. "You are always safe with me, Jane. You have my word."

"I know. Thank you," Jane said with a soft kiss to his lips. "I know, but I..." Jane broke their embrace as her voice trailed off.

"Jane, what are you thinking? What's wrong?" Gabriel asked with worry. "Talk to me, Jane, please."

Although Jane heard and felt his concern for her, she wasn't sure if she could trust herself not to hurt him. Her mind raced with many worries as she walked towards the broken window. One such troublesome thought landed on Damian. Was it possible he followed her to the brewery tonight? He was the only man who drove a truck that she knew of and had enough of a temper to do something like this. But why? Why would he be jealous of Gabriel when he made it perfectly clear months ago that he no longer loved or wanted her. As she recalled the window shattering, Jane remembered hearing the word 'whore' yelled out. Was it meant for her? Why? Maybe it was Brooke who hated her for being with Gabriel tonight? Shaking her head and closing her eyes, Jane hoped that when she opened them again, everything would be as it was. But much to her disappointment, it wasn't, and instead, her reality was flooded with red and blue lights as the police arrived.

"Jane, I'm going to talk to the police. They'll need to talk to you as well," Gabriel stated, then paused and realized she was still scared. He wished he could reassure her all would be ok. Walking to Jane, he placed a tender kiss on her lips. "I'm sorry this happened tonight. I will take care of you. You are safe with me." Gabriel cradled Jane against his chest, holding her still trembling body in his arms. Everything will be ok," he said, giving a kiss on the top of her head before he met the police in the main lobby area.

Jane wrapped her arms around herself, turning back to look outside the shattered window. *Was this all her fault? Was it Damian or perhaps Brooke?* Either way, Jane concluded she didn't want to let Gabriel or the police know she might know who might be responsible, for she feared further harm to Gabriel. Would she lose him if she kept it secret, though? She would never forgive herself if anything happened to him. A shuddering sigh left Jane's chest in an effort to ease the guilt in her heart and pressure in her chest as she pondered what to say. Would Gabriel leave her when he realized drama followed her, making it unbearable to be around her? Would she be alone once again? The storm of wearisome thoughts was relentless as they conjured an evil hex of doubt and shame upon Jane. Looking out the shattered window into a vast, dark nothingness, the only question Jane couldn't let go of, couldn't find an answer for was what was she going to do?

Manufactured by Amazon.ca
Acheson, AB